I0772943

EDEN EMORY
& ASHLEY PINES

NOTE

This is a work of fiction. Names, characters, business, events and incidents are the products of the author's imagination. Any resemblance to actual persons, living or dead, or actual events is purely coincidental.

Before moving forward, please note that the themes in this book can be dark and trigger some people. The themes can include but are not limited to; depictions of torture, choking (nonsexual), choking (sexual), blood play, gore/violence, knife play, weapon of convenience, gun violence, shibari/rope play, overstimulation, orgasm denial, voyeurism (forced and unforced), murder, stabbing, sexual violence, biting, physical altercations, mutilation, mutilation of a corpse, toxic capitalism, getting caught in machinery, drowning, attempted murder, verbal, mental and physical abuse by a parent, crimes of passion, gaslighting, ableist language, misgendering, homophobia, head injury, stalking, transphobia/transphobic language, bugs (mostly cockroaches), rats, animal death (rats), inappropriate use of a baseball bat, cult mentalities, mention of cults/manifestos and active cult behavior, religious paraphernalia, mentions of god/religion, beheading, stabbing, claustrophobic scenarios, being buried alive.

National Suicide Prevention Lifeline
1-800-273-8255
https://suicidepreventionlifeline.org/

National Domestic Violence Hotline
1-800-799-7233
https://www.thehotline.org/

Pronouns & Nicknames

Cam:
    Everyday: They/She
    Family: Daughter
    Lover: Cowboy

Aubrey:
    Everyday: She/Her
    Family: Daughter
    Lover: Peaches / Whore / Temptress

For those who want to be choked out by a yeehaw muscle mommy
with religious trauma.

EDEN EMORY
& ASHLEY PINES

CAM

GAME ON!

I swear Pa thought the fuckin' sun rose just to hear him crow.

My parents boxed me in on either side of the extended leather bench seat, the black town car we'd taken from the hotel way too big for three people.

But that was the thing about my family—they lived and breathed *everything bigger in Texas*—and not just because when we all got together there were damn near enough of us to man a football team. It was all about the *look* of things.

Bigger car? More money.

Never mind that if I lost today we'd go from rooster to feather duster quicker than I could say Rat Race.

Ma squeezed my hand impatiently, and I opened an eye lazily to look at her giant, curled silver hair. Her cherry-painted lips were turned into a frown, talking out of the corner of her mouth.

"Pay attention."

I'd barely registered that Pa was still talking, his performative *praying* of no interest to me. There was a time when I would've hung on his every word. But that was ages ago—before he rebranded the Ranch from a corporation into a church.

Naw, not just *a* church. A fuckin' company in a religious society's clothing. A *Mega Church.*

Fuck me, would I be glad to be out.

I'd played the game better than my siblings, or maybe I was the least indoctrinated since I was able to attend a few classes at the local university once I'd scored out of the Ranch's educational system.

Thank fuck for deprogramming and liberal arts universities.

"And may you, for the glory and honor of your never-ending vengeance, bring Camilla to victory so that we may continue to be heralds of your great message. Amen."

Yeah, not grace. Not goodness.

Vengeance.

Y'see, the Ranch wasn't just a *church*—it was a training facility. A fuckin' expensive one, though incorrectly touted as a free perk for members of the Church. A church whose membership was contingent on the parishioners supplying a cool thirty percent of their income to "tithing."

You hand over thirty percent of your income to us and full control over your little frog spawn, and we'll churn out the most lethal players The Devil's Playground's ever seen. How? Don't worry about it.

God will show them the way.

And by God, they meant brutal, systemic stripping of your entire sense of self to condition you to be able to kill without thinking.

But hey, love and light!

"Amen," Ma and I muttered in unison, hers much more enthusiastic than my own.

If there was a God, I reckoned he'd be none too happy with the way my parents were portraying him. Naw, if anything, I had a feelin' I was in for a *world* of trouble if someone managed to snuff me out today.

"You're ready, Cammy," Ma said in her thick southern drawl, pulling a flat, silver cigarette case from her tan leather handbag. "Best and brightest always come from the Ranch. And y'know why—?"

"Discipline," I interrupted, barely biting back my sigh. But it didn't matter. I'd watched Ma give this speech to five of my siblings before me. It never changed.

"—Discipline. None of that funny individualism stuff they tried to paint you with at that... *secular*..." She said the word like it was dirty. "School of yours. Good old-fashioned family values. That's what makes Weston's a cut above the rest."

"Yes, Ma," I agreed placatingly, my eyes finding the window as she cracked it open, the sunlight pouring in now that there was a gap in the dark tinting.

She lit the butt, cherry lipstick painting a thick print around the filter of her cigarette as she sucked on it, exhaling a steady stream of smoke a few moments later. "Let's hear it then, the Proclamation."

Beside her, Pa wrinkled his nose, thick, black-dyed mustache wiggling. He hated when she smoked in the car. But Ma was nervous, and that meant she'd had a cigarette between her fingers since her eyes popped with the first alarm.

Only pause was to pray, naturally.

Just didn't do for a good, God-fearing woman to be seen abusing substances. Unless those substances were about a quart of whiskey every Christmas Eve since before I was born.

I fought the urge to sigh. *Not this shit again.*

As if growing up with the Games shoved down my throat since I could crawl through the toddler-sized maze that my folks called a playpen wasn't enough, all these reminders in the last few months as I prepared to play in my first Games were really starting to be overkill.

Robotically, though a bit comically given my own accent, I started cycling through the Weston Ranch Manifesto that'd been as good as injected directly into my veins.

"Honor your parents."

If you asked me, stealing directly from the Ten Commandments was a bit tacky, but hey, this was a late-stage capitalistic cult in a church's clothing, I couldn't be that picky. The first, at least, hadn't been edited from the main text. But the other four tenets?

They read more like a wikiHow on how to become a serial killer than pillars for good Samaritanism.

Probably on the account that they were.

"Make yourself an idol in the eyes of the people, for the glory and greatness of God is the center of all celebration."

Hard to push more people into your batshit-crazy cult if they didn't know who you were, I guessed.

"You should refrain from murder," I sighed.

"The rest, Camilla," Ma prompted impatiently.

"Unless unduly necessary. Should you claim a life, make it a show of your faith."

Often shortened at the Ranch to *make a show of it*. Obviously, they couldn't push too hard in our written materials to go out and *kill people*. But in the privacy of our facility? Yeah. We were told to be *lethal*. It was the reason Hide N' Seek was the second most popular event for Ranch alumni.

Idols and murderers with *style*—a perfect recipe for truly lethal Seekers.

Pa hummed appreciatively, smoothing his checked, button-down shirt over his rounded belly. "That's my good girl. Next?"

"You shall not covet. Observe the desires of the Church and obtain them by any means necessary."

"And?"

"Hold nothing above the will of your God."

That is to say, nothing is more important than winning the Games.

Your sole purpose is to bring glory to the family and the Ranch—and get the check that came with it. Because at the end of the day, was there any greater honor than ensuring that the rich continued to get richer? Lining their pockets with filthy, bloody dollar bills and checks from online gambling websites because salvation is *now*.

I scrubbed a hand through my hair, messing up the dark shag.

Part of me was *so* bitter about the way my parents had manipulated and used me and my siblings—not to mention the dozens of other children they'd raised to be murder machines over the years. But I did have to admit, our family record, the *Ranch* record, was unbeatable. A success rate of over ninety-five percent.

Unheard of.

Questioning was just one of the trials of a good devotee. When I made it through this, after I'd brought us into the ninety-sixth success rate percentile... Then I could consider if I was a true believer or not.

This was *God's* chance to show *me* that I hadn't wasted my life on a false prophet. That this was *real*.

"Get the earliest wave ya can," Pa said encouragingly, squeezing my knee. "If yer able, go left first. Statistically, the tougher traps are always to the right."

"And pace yourself," Ma chimed in, taking my hand with the one that wasn't occupied by yet another cigarette. "Pay attention to your surroundings. And for heaven's sake, don't forget to—"

"Smile big for the cameras," I finished with a charming, lopsided grin I'd practiced in the mirror hundreds of times. "What, y'all don't trust that I got this?"

"Naw, we trust you," Pa said, the corners of his dark eyes crinkling with his toothy, gaped smile. Man always could eat a cob of corn through a picket fence. "Always been our little athlete, Cam. Ain't none that could get through the simulations faster than you."

I pushed away the warm, preening feelings in my gut. It didn't do me any good to *want* my parents to be proud of me... And yet a voice whispered in the back of my mind, *Honor your parents.*

When I was barely to Pa's knee, I couldn't wait for my turn in the Games. My siblings graduated the training program one by one, the entire family piling into a town car just like this to drop them off at the train station to the island. As viewers, we would take one of the ferries—and get ice cream. Not a bad consolation prize.

For Hope's Games, five years earlier, when I was thirteen, I'd been so jealous of her that I'd cried the entire way to the ferry car park. *How dare she go without me?* I remembered thinking. Teenage Cam was outraged that their favorite sister had abandoned them in the viewing area while she went off to make the family proud.

It was supposed to be *my* job.

But now that my turn was finally here? It felt a bit like bread that'd been left on the counter overnight—stale. Not disconnected in the way that things you're looking forward to often do. Like how graduation is supposed to be this big, life-changing moment, and really it's just a hot, sweaty day in an auditorium with faulty air conditioning and far too many mouth-breathin' hogs.

Naw, this was something else.

Like disillusionment, or whatever.

I was just another checkbox in a long line of Legacy babies Ma and Pa had reared for the sole purpose of creating champions. No more or less important than a prize-winning pig they'd been feeding since spring. People just took a little longer to prime.

The insignia on my jacket, a pair of golden interconnected horseshoes with six diamonds fitted into them—real ones, not those lab-grown fakes—had room for one more gem to be fitted into the material. It was my spot. And a silent warning that the only way I was allowed to come out of the maze was as a winner.

Fine, or as a corpse.

Billy's diamond had been pressed out of his ashes. The only loss in our entire family's history in four generations.

An embarrassment.

However the fuck I felt about the Games, I knew one thing— I wasn't no fuckin' embarrassment.

I'm going to win.

The car slowed to a stop as the train station came into view, halting at the rounded bottom of the drop-off zone. Concrete steps sandwiched between elegant flower beds led toward the modern platform. A few uniformed security guards lingered by the glass sliding doors, made necessary by the quickly accumulating crowd, desperate to get a first glimpse at the people that, in a few hours' time, could go from run-of-the-mill players to *champions*.

Ma flicked her cigarette onto the pavement and rolled up her window at the first camera flash, raising a bottle-blonde eyebrow. "Teeth check."

I smiled big, turning my head in the car's dim lights for her to inspect for stray food or missed plaque. She nodded, humming in approval before reaching out to fluff my hair into devil-may-care perfection.

Pa huffed. "Betsy, leave 'em be for Christ's sake."

She rolled her eyes, ignoring him. "We'll be in the gallery, same—"

"Spot as every year. Yeah, Ma, I know. Now let me out of this car to kiss babies and make the Ranch some money."

Pa offered me a checkered red and white bandana with the same insignia as my jacket, and I took it, quickly using it to shine my silver belt buckle. "I was worried that with you going off to that fancy school you might come home to us with all these ideas in your head. But you never fail to impress me, Camilla. Congratulations."

Not good luck.

Luck would mean that there was a chance I wouldn't win. Naw, as far as he was concerned, I just needed to walk in there and claim my trophy.

He was probably right.

I tucked the handkerchief into my pocket, tipping an invisible hat to my parents as I opened the door of the car to an explosion of screams and applause.

His worries about my newfangled modern secular values were only half right anyways. Questioning. That was the word I kept telling myself.

Turns out it wasn't so easy to walk away from values your

parents spent your entire life beating into you. It took a bit more than a Poli-Sci lecture and a couple well-positioned classes on propaganda.

Thanking my lucky stars for the heavy ropes keeping the crowd back from the steps, I waved with that same practiced smile. "Aw shucks, all this for little ol' me?"

"Camilla," Ma started sternly, "Make sure you talk about the Ranch—"

"Uh-huh," I said distractedly as I glanced up at the digitized screens by the doors. The first event, Hide N' Seek, had wrapped up a couple of hours ago as the sun had started to rise, the inarguable winners, wh1te_r4bb1t and k1llerKohl_ waving and smiling in their after-event press coverage.

Christ, they let anything be a hair color nowadays, I thought of the femme's bright teal locks.

"In and out, no bullshit, no getting distracted being *nice*—" Pa started.

"Got it," I interrupted, winking at his look of exasperation before shutting the door with a loud click.

They'd get their time in front of the cameras when they arrived at the arena. This was *my* moment.

I turned to face the crowd, the smallest of my siblings standing at five foot nine as I raised my hand to wave, smile fixed in place as the barrage of flashes blinded me for several seconds.

The last thing I needed was the embarrassment of being the second sibling to fail out of the maze. Naw, there was no choice. I was gonna go in there and win.

Even if I was the gentlest of the brood—the only one to consistently fail the humanity-based stress tests. Not that I saw how that was *my* fault. How the fuck was I supposed to just shoot a dog that I raised from a pup?

Fucking insanity. But which one of us wasn't a bit loose in the mind and morals? I was willingly walking to my possible death after all.

Didn't matter. I was the last of us. It was time to finish things off with a bang.

And, for the record, the dog in question—Mutty Buddy, a hilarious play on works for a ten-year-old—was living out her golden years chasing around chickens on the farm.

I moved to grab a black Sharpie from one of the women waiting in the crowd with a playful wink. Uncapping the marker with my teeth, I used it to sign several notebooks, posters from my pre-show Legacy coverage, Ranch-branded T-shirts and hoodies, and even one exceptionally well-rounded breast.

I added a little heart to the end of that one. C'mon now, I might've been representing a Mega Church, but I wasn't no saint.

If anything, I was a sinner through and through.

They weren't just my fans. They were fans of my siblings. Of my whole *family*. Of the Ranch, where my parents trained class after class of positively fatal athletes with a legacy of winning every. Single. Time.

Best fuckin' training facility in the country—and I was its heir.

Well, sixth in line.

Sorry, Billy, miss you every day. Even if you were a goddamn disappointment.

No matter how I felt about the Devil's Playground, I was gonna get that fuckin' diamond. And it wouldn't be because I was rottin' in a body bag.

Game on.

Aubrey

Save it for the Games.

Being from the city during the Devil's Playground was a bit like being at ground zero for the Super Bowl, only on steroids. People you'd barely noticed before were suddenly forced down your throat at every turn. A feeling made even more obvious now that it was my classmates and friends being pushed into the spotlight instead of airbrushed strangers or older siblings.

Fucking unbearable.

I leaned back in the salon chair while my stylist worked at curling my hair, her deep, umber skin reflecting back at me in the mirror.

She was beautiful, and under different circumstances I might've complimented her long lilac braids or sparkling golden eyeshadow. But not today.

Today, I needed to make sure that everything was *perfect*.

Especially me.

My eyes left the mirror to find a familiar face reading from a teleprompter on the small screen of a tablet I'd commandeered. There, my friend, Victoria Miller, spoke her lines like she was being held at knifepoint.

Vic's eyes moved away from her script, looking straight into the camera as she smiled, her straight white teeth almost glowing under the lights in the studio.

"Whoever kills Hiram will get paid out a million dollars, regardless of whether you win the Games. Hell, I'll even cut the check myself. If you can make me laugh while you're doing it, I'll double it," she said with a smile so bloodthirsty—*feral*—that I'd never have expected from Miss Polly Pocket, the *cheer captain* herself.

I couldn't help the giggle that escaped my lips.

Damn, she knows how to play the game.

Out of the arena and still trying to cut down her enemies... An interesting choice of target, too. Hiram Wolff, an Architect and father to two nightmare children—well, one nightmare child now. Vic had seen to that in the arena. I had known Dylan from the parties he'd thrown at the Wolff mansion, if you could call them that. If anything, they'd just been an excuse to try and bully his then girlfriend into some wholly unenjoyable sex.

Dudes with attitudes like Dylan were *never* any good at giving head. That and their general lack of overall appeal really solidified the whole softball-loving lifestyle I was curating for myself.

Friend of Ellen, if you get me.

But the youngest Wolff sibling, Kohl? They were barely worth notice at all.

A million dollars, two for a laugh.

With a payday like that, even *I* was tempted to try my hand at hunting him down... Fuck, maybe I would after I dealt with *her*. I didn't really plan on winning this thing anyway—just making sure she was headed home in a plasticized body bag with her address scrawled hastily on top.

It was important to have goals in life. SMART goals at that.

Specific, in that she would be dead as a doornail and have a pathetic, miserable funeral with her alcoholic mother ugly crying into her father's polyester tie.

Measurable, since it was just one teeny tiny murder.

Achievable, as there was no way that lazy cunt could outrun

me after I'd spent the entire summer allowing the local CrossFit gym bootcamps to rock my shit into the best shape of my life.

Relevant, since, truly, what was more relevant than the Devil's Playground? It was all anyone would be talking about for the foreseeable future.

And, perhaps the most important one, time-bound—by the end of the day she'd be finished and I'd be free of ever having to look at her shitty tape-in extensions ever again.

Even just the thought of that *bitch* has me threatening to teeter off the edge with rage.

You'll get yours, just you wait.

Gold-shadow girl paused, the curling iron held aloft as she watched the screen of the tablet over my shoulder, a sort of proud smirk curving her full lips.

I hadn't expected to see anyone from my school on the big screen, even if there were a few Legacies in my class. Vic hadn't even bothered to do the press junket that having a parent who won the Games got you, so I figured her plan was to ditch. Especially since she was always going on and *on* about how the Games were just a modern-day Colosseum. A way for the ultra-rich to get richer and the poor to suffer in the hopes of changing their circumstances.

Yawn. Sounded like a bunch of proletariat bullshit to me.

Either buck up or shut up, really. We all signed up to play. It wasn't like you were being forced into it.

Still, out of all of the idiots we knew, Vic was the one to actually do it.

Win.

It wasn't that much of a surprise, once you got over the shock of her playing at all—a *Legacy*, not to mention by far the brightest of our graduating class? Yeah, Miller had the grit and talent needed to take on a game like *Hide N' Seek*.

And, to my delight, a penchant for cruelty. Catching the end of her game on the way here was a masterclass on not judging a book by its cover.

Kohl chokes me harder than that when we fuck, she said, and it almost made me laugh again to think about it. Fucking. Vicious.

Beside her, the erotic asphyxiator themselves, Kohl, played with Victoria's fingers as she spoke, their mouth slanted into a relaxed smile.

Now *this*? This was a surprise.

I'd seen them lingering around her at school when they thought we weren't looking. Their obvious crush was amusing, if not a bit pathetic. I mean, come on! Your *brother's* girlfriend? A cheerleader and the school freak? Could you be more of a cliche?

Last I checked, this wasn't the fucking Breakfast Club, and if it were, I can sure as shit tell you that Molly Ringwald never would've dared to even *think* about dying her hair that color.

Still, it was entertaining, so I'd let it slide. No reason to deny myself life's simple pleasure of watching a friendless loser lust after a girl totally out of their league, y'know? But seeing them on the screen together? That veered straight into *interesting* territory.

I wished I could've caught more of them during Hide N' Seek. The glimpses that I'd managed were nothing in comparison to the highlight reel they were playing now. Blow after blow. Murder after murder.

That fight in the Mirror Maze? Photo. Fucking. Finish.

And to be invited to commentate on the next event? In the same tournament year? *Living legends.*

Didn't matter, though. I'd get in there, kill the cunt, and be home in time to watch the entire weekend on my PVR with some pizza and champagne. Usually, I'd go for some wine coolers, but I figured I could spring for the good stuff since I was about to become a millionaire.

It's the little things.

I'd gotten to the island early in the hopes of catching a bit of the competition live, but the useless bitch they'd assigned to do my makeover was taking her sweet time. At least the highlights were impressive—it was all anyone was talking about in the dressing room. Well, at least the stylists were. Most of the incoming players for Rat Race were either watching the footage, pale and uncomfortable as they realized it was absolutely too late to back out, or, like me, trying to enjoy some peace before the next few stressful hours.

No amount of deep breathing exercises or mindful meditation was going to make running for your life any easier, though. Maybe I should've brought a stress ball.

Snatches of conversation floated over to me with the distinct air of gossiping about people so far out of your social strata it should've been criminal.

It was pathetic, really. The way these stylists would help the machine run, dressing us up pretty to ship us out to our events without ever having stepped into the arena themselves. Awfully easy to talk about how much faster you'd have shot the person trying to drown you when you'd never had a gun in your hand.

I fucking hate cowards.

"I did theirs," the stylist said, her manicured finger moving to point at Kohl on the small screen. "They'd look good in just about anything, but absolutely killed the crop top. You should try something—"

"Did I ask for your opinion?" I questioned with a sickly sweet smile, turning in my chair to look at her with a raised eyebrow.

I needed as many eyes on me as possible tonight. As if I were going to chance a *stranger's* judgment on what I should be wearing. No, I'd be choosing my own look, thank you.

The stylist's smile dropped, disappointment flashing across her face for a split second before her hand tightened around my hair. The curling iron paused mid-air as she digested my words, the heat radiating off the black barrel to warm my face. To be safe, I tugged away the strand of blonde hair she was holding, leaning away.

"Let's not get excited with that iron, hm?" I suggested in an irritated purr. "My face is worth more than your house."

The last fucking thing I needed was a giant burn to tote around while about a thousand cameras tracked my every move. If

I had to spend the next fifty years watching playback footage looking like I lost a fight with a candle, I was going to fucking lose it.

She opened her mouth to speak, but I beat her to it, grabbing the iron out of her hand. Turning back to the mirror with that same, vapid smile.

"My sponsors want a specific look," I chirped, regaining my composure and transforming back into the doe-eyed doll I'd been hired to play. My gaze caught hers in the mirror, my sick satisfaction at her obvious offense evident. "You don't mind, do you?"

She let out a shocked gasp that I ignored, beginning to deal with my hair. Passing the hot iron from root to mids before I lightly curled the ends. It didn't take long for her to fuck off to go find me something to wear—not that it really mattered what it was, as long as it matched the heavy, patch-covered leather motocross-style jacket I needed to wear into the arena.

Part of my contract was wearing my sponsor's logo.

That was the thing about Rat Race versus something like Hide N' Seek—since the mortality rate was lower, there was less money in the game itself. Most of the major players built their fortunes off deals with companies, and for girls like me who had an existing social media presence? This was just another commercial shoot.

I'd wear the jacket, cross the finish line at any point, and collect my check. And if I was in the top ten percent, the payout was even bigger.

Paired with the added benefit that I'd finally get to set that useless cunt's teeth on the curb and stomp, it was a win-win.

Using the mirror, I looked around at the competitors being styled in nearby booths. Though there were many contestants inside the large, tent-like room, the person I was most anxious to see was still missing.

I sighed in exasperation.

"Soon," I whispered to myself, focusing on making my bangs as bouncy as possible.

In truth, the sponsors didn't give a fuck about how my hair or makeup was done, but I had a brand, and I wasn't going to let some hapless beauty school reject make me look like a clown on international television.

No, the corporate boozers that I'd effectively signed my life away to were lucky I'd chosen something from their catalog at all. Given my existing audience, having me wear their logo across my back was the best promo opportunity they could ask for. I'd be at the top of the leaderboard almost instantly as my followers signed on to watch me play, meaning I'd have even more visibility to bring in new eyes.

Thank fuck for my publicist for not having to deal with any of the bullshit back and forth. Nothing irritated me more than when a company reached out on my socials with some fake-ass perfectly curated *Hey girly!!* message to internet-beg me to wear their cheap, child labor-made jewelry.

You always did better with me by sending PR first and asking questions later—at least then I'd already know if I liked your product enough to try and convince my flock of overconsumers to buy the next greatest serum or this season's must-have lipstick.

Cue eye roll.

After the game, once I made sure to mention that Mantene was the reason my hair was so long and shiny—it wasn't, half of this shit was extensions, K-tips obviously—they'd all be kissing my feet. Not to mention sending me a fucking Birkin stuffed with cash and an all-inclusive vacation to Barbados as a thank you.

You're welcome, cunts.

My useless stylist finally reemerged, wheeling a rack of clothes overfilled to bursting with options for me to wear inside the maze. I set the curling iron aside, rotating the chair and hopping out, moving to thumb through it with vicious efficiency.

Outside the Games, flashy clothes weren't really my thing. Well, unless they'd been sent to me for free. But for this? I needed something loud, exciting.

Eye-catching.

Purple, yellow, black... I was almost halfway through the rack, muttering irritated *noes* to myself as garment after garment sailed by on the shrieking metal rail. Before long, I was already at the end of my options.

"Do I have to do everything around here?" I snapped, shoving the rolling rack aside and into the stylist with more force than necessary.

Stomping toward the back in my socked feet, I paused as I saw another entrant's stylist holding up a sparkly, cropped two-piece set with a mini skirt and built-in shorts in hot pink.

Perfect.

The Devil's Playground were *games,* after all. Reality TV with a deadly twist. That meant there were main characters, fan favorites, and villains. I was going to be all three.

I might've had a single motive for participating, but that didn't mean I had to look or behave like every other random loser who decided to play.

Fuck that, I'm a star.

That meant I didn't follow trends. I made them.

I elbowed my way through the tightly packed room, swiping the outfit out of the other player's hands before they could touch the vibrant material.

"Uh, hello, bitch? That's mine!" the brunette whined, her long, straight hair falling over her shoulder.

I rolled my eyes, lunging forward and barking loudly at her until she backed up, wide eyes finding the floor.

"What the hell you freak?"

She pushed herself up to a standing position and whipped the dirt off her outfit.

"I don't like people touching what's mine." She rolled her eyes at that.

"Fine keep it, just know the pink will clash with your blood when you kill yourself," she said with a scoffHer ego obviously bruised.

"Thought so," I said with another one of those award-winning smiles and a wink. "Thanks. I think blue is more your color anyway."

Turning quickly enough that my long blonde hair made contact with her round, moon-like face, I returned to my station to see my stylist throwing her hands up.

"Well, I never! Just—style yourself then!" she huffed, storming away.

"I plan on it!" I called after her, changing quickly and sitting back in the chair to do my makeup. "If you want to help, find me some fucking shoes!"

Speakers crackled overhead, the Devil's Playground theme song warning the room at large that an announcement was coming. A hush fell over the crowd, eyes turning upward as though they could obtain the information quicker by sight alone.

I grabbed a liquid liner pen from the stylist's kit, making quick work darkening my lash line. For the most part, I'd already done my makeup before arriving, my permanent lash extensions putting in the work to make me look put together despite the rest of my face being relatively light.

Dewy and fresh was the goal, given I'd probably sweat most of it off in the maze anyway. The last thing I needed was racoon eyes, even if I'd be wearing a mask.

"Players!" a cheery, computer-generated voice called. "Lots will be assigned momentarily through a randomized process. Please refer to your trackers for instructions and proceed to your gate promptly."

Randomized process. As-fucking-if. It was well known that the so-called random algorithm took into account how likely you were to beat the maze, potential popularity with viewers, and your Legacy status when it came to choosing how early you'd be able to enter the arena.

Which meant that finally, *finally*, I was about to effortlessly beat *her* at something. There wasn't a chance in hell that I'd be anything but first heat. Massive social following, physically fit, conventionally attractive, and... Well, I wasn't a fucking Legacy, but what did that matter?

I didn't need to have a genetic advantage to know that this was going to be child's play.

Pings filled the room like popping bubbles, players letting out excited noises as they read out their assigned lots. My tracker remained lifeless on my wrist, not a ping or a vibration in sight.

I frowned. Maybe it was faulty? Bringing the device up to my face, my frown quickly turned into a scowl as the screen lit, the cheery yellow waiting smiley face greeting me like a taunt.

Maybe they're starting from the last lot, I told myself, trying to keep calm.

The stylist returned with a pair of platform boots that I tugged on as ping after ping went through the room.

I counted the rounds of sound.

One.

With my boots secured, I returned to the mirror, using my nail to sharpen my liner impatiently before dousing my face again with setting spray. This shit needed to stay put for hours of running. If I could, I'd have brought a powder puff in there with me too.

Little Miss *Vogue* sauntered past, scowling at me in what would've been her clothes. "See you in there, Barbie," she snarked, dragging her thumb across her throat in an obvious threat.

I laughed, waving her off. "Good luck, Skipper." Ah yes, Barbie's much less cool brunette friend. Seriously, hadn't she gotten the memo? Blondes had way more fun. "You'll need it."

"We'll see about that."

If I had time after dealing with *her*, maybe I'd deal with that one too before crossing the finish line.

Two, I counted as more pings filled the room.

There was no reason for me to be anything other than first lot. So what the *fuck* was going on?

I curled a few more strands of hair before placing the iron

down, applying a quick layer of hair spray, and smoothing down any flyaways.

Three.

Anxious whispers began to break out through the rapidly thinning crowd. There were only five heats in Rat Race, the fifth entering the race dead last—so much harder to win not only because you were so far behind the first group, but also because the rest of the players had first pick on any helpful items. Like water, weapons, or first-aid supplies.

Four.

My tracker vibrated, the soft melodic ping chiming happily. The number four flashed back at me in the mirror, my mouth dropping open in shocked horror.

Four?!

How the fuck did they decide that I was in lot four?!

Second to last?!

It was an insult. It was the Architects telling me I wasn't flashy enough to be put in the first few lots. That I was fucking ordinary.

Anger boiled inside me and was only exacerbated by the knowledge that *she* was likely in an earlier heat.

Fuck, fuck, fuck!

If I wasn't the first, she was sure to be. It always happened that way. No matter how hard I tried, she was always one better. Just a breath out of reach.

I could win the Nobel fucking Peace Prize and this cunt would manage to be the first woman on Mars or some other equally insane bullshit.

And if by some miracle she'd been knocked down a peg? She would damn well make sure that I was knocked down even further.

Always a step ahead. Always outshining me.

I'd splatter her fucking brain for a mile.

This. *This* was the benefit of being born a fucking Legacy. Of getting a golden ticket to the easy life.

I let out a primal scream, feeling the rush of anger explode through my body. Taking the curling iron into my hand by its handle, I threw it into the mirror, creating a cascade of sparkling glass fragments. What remained of its surface was spiderwebbed with cracks, distorting the perfect image it reflected back at me.

"Don't destroy The Company's property," a guard yelled from the exit.

My returning glare could've peeled paint, my lip curling into a vicious sneer.

"Why don't you come over here and—" I started, only to be spoken over.

It nearly threw me over the edge. But the last thing I was going to do was get disqualified for attacking a fucking glorified babysitter.

"Save it for the Games," he called, the smile pulling at his thin lips, baring his overcrowded teeth. The expression itself caused another wave of frustration to go through me. He looked at me like he knew what my fate would be once I left this room.

He expects me to die.

Joke's on him. The stupid fucker only saw the image I created for the cameras, nothing more. But that thought wasn't comforting. It only made me angrier.

My watch flashed again with a countdown, warning that I only had half an hour before I needed to be at my gate. I pulled my jacket from the back of the chair, shrugging into it as I turned for the door.

"Waivers have already been signed, princess. There's no backing out now," he called mockingly.

I let out a laugh.

Back out? As fucking if.

With a final look in the shattered mirror, I fluffed my hair. Most of the other players had already cleared out, save for the last lot, easily identifiable by their irritated, shell-shocked expressions as the reality of their situation started to sink in.

Fucking cannon fodder.

And I was nearly one of them.

I could feel their gazes on me as I flipped the guard the bird on the way by, picking up a glowing pink mask from a rack of colorful options. "See you in the winner's circle."

Even if I could, I wouldn't back out. I came here for a reason. Nothing scared me. Not the risk of being killed or whatever the fuck else awaited me in that maze.

I was here for *her*.

And I wouldn't be leaving until I had my hands wrapped around her throat.

CAM

I won't hurt you, sugar.

I adjusted the red and white checked bandana around my neck—the very same one Pa handed me on my way out of the car. Where the costumes for Hide N' Seek were mostly a mix of ultra-modern, sleek, cyberpunk styles, the clothes for the maze were different. Gussied up, given that we didn't need to try to blend into mechanical equipment or tuck ourselves behind abandoned bumper cars.

The point was to be seen. Often, loudly, and ideally looking sexy while we ran for our lives.

Roosters gonna crow, y'know.

My stylist had gone for something subtle—not. Fitted wide-leg jeans and cowboy boots paired with a tight tank top that showed off my tattoos and muscular arms. Given I'd grown up in Texas—on the Ranch no less—it was fitting.

Especially the understated black cowboy hat. All I needed was to find myself some rope in the maze and I'd be ready to go—a veritable John Wayne.

Westons usually ended up in some form of cowboy attire, and I wasn't the exception to the rule. Though I could've done without the star embellishments on my ass, even if they were black, made to mostly blend in with the denim. It still felt a bit... showboaty. For my taste at least. Ma would be thrilled.

The stands around us were filled with people, lifted five feet in the air and separated from us with an electrified force field to stop players from crawling into it—well, and spectators from throwing helpful items down. That was a big problem back in the '76 Games. A player had been slipped a loaded handgun right before they walked into the maze.

PR disaster. Talk about shootin' fish in a barrel.

Excited conversations filtered down to us in the pit, where we waited for the gate numbers to be called. Aside from the heats, we also had to worry about where in the maze we'd enter, but that could wait a minute.

I hunted the stands for my parents, finding Ma n' Pa seated in their private box with the rest of the family brood. Nearly a decade of winners all within a ten-foot radius.

By the end of tonight I'd be one of them, or die trying.

Hope sat at the front of the box, bouncing my nephew, Micah, on her lap and helping the round-faced toddler wave down to me.

I waved back, my red-lit mask dangling from the fingers of my free hand.

Wearing it was about as useless as gum on a boot heel with my tattoos uncovered. I was easily identifiable to everyone both inside and outside of the arena if they'd watched even a minute of the pre-game coverage.

Wasn't no surprise either that I'd been put into the first heat of Runners to enter the maze.

The underground dome was built a bit like half of a football stadium, a large semicircle of stands and private boxes separated from the game floor filled with contestants. We entered through a concrete tunnel built below the seats onto the pitch—a field of synthetic grass and slightly raised metal platforms.

I reckoned I'd be in the first heat given my status. I'd be one of the most watched streams of the day.

The last Weston.

The end of an era.

Like with Hide N' Seek, it was important to score yourself a dedicated audience, and quickly. Though gifts were less common in the underground tunnels of the maze, their messages could be the difference between making the right decision or one that left you dead as a roadside possum.

An alarm blared overhead, the warm-toned white lights turning red for several pulses to warn us it was about time to begin.

My eyes found my parents again, noticing that Pa was waving down onto the pitch—but not to me. My stomach knotted as my gaze moved to follow his, landing on a familiar broad-shouldered back.

What.

In.

Hell.

Players stopped piddlin' around pretty quick, heading for their designated platforms, our watches indicating what platform we'd use to enter the arena.

My watch flashed with my gate number—five—damn near as close to the middle as you could get between the seven available. I moved to stand on the pressurized platform, taking the five short steps two at a time. There was a gap between us and the metal gate, its jaw-like doors sealed tightly shut.

After the seven doors opened and we entered, they'd shut again, the next heat of players queueing up to enter the maze.

I hunted the crowd for those shoulders again, my face heating with anger as Elijah's easy smile met my furious stare. He waved a hand in my direction, like the stupid son of a bitch was meant to be here.

It was a Ranch rule—on the year Weston kids entered the maze, the other initiates' children sat out. Saved us from the nightmare of friendly fire.

Wasn't so good for the congregation or the pocketbook if Ma and Pa let their students enter with us so we could kill 'em.

So why the fuck is he here?

Did Pa really not trust me to bring the win home for us?

I rounded the platform, my eyes still on Elijah where he waited at the platform for gate four, until I stood at the front. I expected complaints from the other Runners, but it turned out there were some benefits to this whole Legacy thing. No one bothered, or maybe was willin', to say anything to me.

Largely, the other players were already breaking off into groups. The randomized heat system was interesting, making it so that even the best and brightest were mingled with nobodies and underdogs. Made for a good mix when we crossed into the arena.

Once the catwalks below raised, the doors would open, letting us into the maze. The spectators would watch the rest of the event through holographic screens, with the Architects—game designers who decided everything from the theme to the traps that were designed to kill us—choosin' which feeds were interestin' enough for mass viewership on a rotation.

I slid my mask down over my face, stretching out my legs as the Runners around me began to damn near vibrate with excitement, forming groups and making allies they'd quickly turn on if given the chance.

Now listen, I wasn't no PKer—player killer. I wanted a good, clean game.

Even if I did have half a mind to hunt Elijah down for daring to enter the arena during my year.

Still, I wasn't looking to make best buddies down here. Teams were statistically more likely to make it to the final, but they also came with a whole slew of risks.

More trouble than it was worth, I'd say.

Naw, if I had it my way, I'd be in and out. Lonely as a fuckin' tumbleweed.

But, given we were smooshed together like sardines, I couldn't help but overhear their plans.

"My dad has a contact," a player with a glowing burnt sienna mask whispered behind me. "He said just keep going to the right. It's like a big circle."

Another with a teal mask laughed—a thin, nasally noise that pricked at my ears uncomfortably.

"I think he's just trying to get you killed, bro."

"He's not! I'm telling you it's a reliable—"

"*Sure* he is," a feminine voice jeered. "Just like when your dad's *friend* told you to 'invest' your money into an *up-and-coming clinically trialed MDMA facility* that just so happened to be his bank account?"

Sienna spluttered. "Calla, that was a whole fucking different thing—I mean it, this is legit."

A scoff from Teal. "As if, listen, Marco, I'd follow your half-baked advice—"

"See!" Marco—Burnt Sienna, I guessed—said in triumph.

"If," interrupted Teal, "And that's a big if, we hadn't won the heat lottery."

"Heat lottery?" asked Calla. "What the fuck are you on about?"

"Idiots," scoffed Teal. "Don't you see those tattoos? I'd recognize those cowboy classics anywhere. That's Camilla Weston. I'd bet my fucking life on it."

You may have to, I thought, glad that my face was hidden behind a glowing red mask. I really didn't need or want an entourage.

"Fine," snapped Marco, obviously put out. "I say we follow cowgirl, then. If you think she knows what she's doing..."

I couldn't help the smirk that tugged at my lips.

I do. Didn't give up my entire childhood to prepare for my debut at the Games for nothing.

The pressure not to let my family down was enormous. If I were being honest, I'd admit that the possibility of coming close to last was weighing on me like three-hundred-pound Uncle

Kenney on that goddamn Shetland pony of his. Damn near broke the old girl's back a time or two.

But that can't happen, I reminded myself firmly, flexing my fingers. *I won't let it.*

Especially not when they'd sent in a fucking backup. When I won this game, I reckoned Pa and I were due for one hell of a shouting match.

Ultimately, how I felt about this circus wasn't important. My worries, nerves? Those needed to be locked up tight.

A legacy four generations in the making rode on this. My failure, destroyin' the last chance we had at a final jewel in the horseshoe that was my family's incredible legacy in the arena? Yeah, the only way I'd let that happen was if I were comin' home in a casket. It didn't matter what rode on this. Didn't matter if I was about to make the family look bad.

A little part of me, the same part that'd cried when Hope went off to her Games, wanted to win for *me*.

Make yourself an idol in the eyes of the people, for the glory and greatness of God is the center of all celebration. Nothing before the will of your God.

I adjusted the hat on my head, rubbing a hand up my bare tattoos.

An idol. Beyond a celebrity, something wholly untouchable. *Mythic.*

A livin' legend.

That's what I'd be when I did this, the final push in my family's meteoric rise into the upper echelon of the elite who built their fortune winnin'.

I pushed away the worries from outside the island, the concept of failure ceasing to exist for me as my focus narrowed on the doors just ahead.

The cheers and shouts from the crowd faded into a blanket of white noise, barely more important than the drone of cicadas in the July heat.

It's just me and the maze. That's it. That's all I had to focus on, I reminded myself as I jogged in place, trying to warm my muscles that'd gone stiff while I sat patiently in the stylist's chair. *Forget everything else.*

The alarm blared, red light filling the room and flashing as the ten-second countdown began, the lit walkways rising slowly as the gates began to open like great sets of crocodile jaws, allowing for the first precious look into the dungeon that'd be my home until I managed to find my way out.

A rat in the trap.

The first corridor went on for about twenty meters before it hit a dead end, warning me that I'd need to make a choice early on. I half hoped that it wouldn't, forcing me onto a certain path.

But, given the number of players assigned to my gate with about ten of us standing in close quarters, I had to guess the first turn would be a *T* to try and split up the pack.

The flashes of cameras were blinding, more frequent the closer the short runway got to clickin' into place. Around me, the other Runners were restless, stirrin' and shiftin' into places that would allow them the best chance of being one of the first people in the maze.

A wave of noise, the crackle of static—an aesthetic choice, given the quality of the sound equipment used—as the Devil's Playground theme song began to play.

The watch at my wrist buzzed, breaking my concentration and pulling my focus.

West_won: *Congratulations, Cam.*

Pa's message should've sent a bolt of pride through me as the announcement began, the Architects using the familiar, chipper AI-generated voice to communicate with the Runners and spectators. Instead, bitterness fueled my thoughts.

"Welcome to Devil's Playground: State Fair, sponsored by

The Company! For those of you joining after Hide N' Seek, welcome back! Our second event of the weekend, Rat Race, is due to begin in a few moments. But first, The Company would like to remind you of a few key rules..."

Overhead, the holographic screens that'd been cyclin' through ads just moments ago flickered and changed. Images of darkened corridors passing by so quickly it was difficult to get a grip of what we were lookin' at. At its center was a running countdown, one hundred and twenty seconds and countin'.

"Runners are permitted to enter the arena for a period of sixty seconds once the timer reaches zero. The timer will then reset to give the next round of contestants ample time to prepare to enter the maze. The Company would like to remind you to be courteous to your fellow Runners. Though not expressly forbidden, we do remind you that killing contestants does not assist in the scoring of Rat Race."

There was a shuffle, another nasally laugh coming from behind me. "Won't stop us, though, will it?"

"As Runners, your objective is simple: reach the end of the maze. The player with the fastest time will earn the most completion bonus points. However, speed isn't the only way to become a champion of this game. There are markers placed around the arena, tracked by your watches, that will add to your score over time. Please ensure you are paying attention to the ranking board, easily accessible by saying 'Rank' to your tracker."

I glanced down at the watch in question. What the cheerful little voice failed to mention? Your view count made all the difference in your point score too. The more viewers, the more *everything* you did was worth.

"If you have any questions, you may contact an Architect via your tracker's call function. Good luck, and remember—" The rest of the machine's message was drowned by a roar of applause erupting through the stadium.

"Play hard! Win, win!" the crowd chanted, my own shout lost to the well of noise.

Rat Race was technically easy, and thank fuck for that since strategy was not my strong suit. Get in. Get out. Don't die. Simple as that. It wasn't a mind game like Truth or Dare. Or a game of allies and betrayal like Hide N' Seek.

Simple. So long as someone didn't decide to interfere with my plans for their own amusement.

It wasn't unheard of in the Games. People joined for a reason, and it wasn't always money. Sometimes it was as simple as being able to get away with things they never could on the outside.

The timer hit ten seconds, and the players and spectators began to chant.

Ten.

There was no turning back.

Nine.

Was that the last time I'd see Hope and the baby?

Eight.

If they were given the chance, would the Runners behind me kill me?

Seven.

Were other players the most dangerous thing I'd find in the maze?

Six.

Was I going to have to kill Elijah?

Five.

Honor your parents.

Four.

Make yourself an idol.

Three.

Make a show of it.

Two.

At all costs, for the glory of God.

One.

Play hard. Win, win.

The lights flashed before bathing us in green light, alerting us that it was time to enter the maze. The doors sat open and waitin', the moment I'd been training my entire life for here within the blink of an eye. My heart beat so fast that it felt like I could cough it up as I stared down the thin runway into the maze, the sound of heavy footfalls echoing as players began to run across the walkway and through the doors.

I hesitated. First in didn't always mean first out.

A few years ago, the first person into the maze was crisped up like a deep-fried turkey the second they crossed the threshold, stumbling over a tripwire that ignited a flamethrower meant to cull the herd within the first few seconds of the game.

Two large, hulking mascs—a well-rounded polite individual couldn't assume pronouns in these trying, post-apocalyptic times —and two femmes, the smaller, more skittish-looking one trailing several steps behind the others, rounded me to dash up our runway, entering the maze.

I wasn't far behind them, my boots clanging against the metal walkway with every step until I crossed the threshold into the maze itself.

The noise that I'd become used to—shuffling from hundreds of feet, anxious whispers and yells from the crowd overhead— dulled with every step into the corridor. Deafening, oppressive silence followed, the absence of many voices and sudden dampened noise of my boots against concrete making me feel off balance.

Surprisingly disorienting.

A whoop of laughter up ahead warned that the Runners I'd let pass had already come in contact with their first obstacle, or at least I guessed so. The noise wasn't joyful. It was strained, full of panic and anxiety.

As I came up to the first fork in the road, my watch dinged.

Hopel3ss: *Left.*

· · ·

A smirk tugged at the corner of my mouth. Leave it to my favorite sister to point me in the right direction early. I took the left passage, hurrying through foot over foot of smooth gray stone.

It was like being in a sensory desert after all of the color and noise a moment ago. Like all the joy had been leached out of the world, leaving it barren and lifeless. We'd prepared for this sensation back at the Ranch—one of the most important things about Rat Race was your ability to mitigate the discomfort that came with the sudden shift of input. Far too many Runners let themselves get all out of sorts right out of the gate, losing track of their whereabouts and making it more difficult to get out of the maze.

What I didn't expect—what surprised even me—was the unshakable feelin' that I was being *watched*. And not just by the thousands of cameras built to view every square inch of this place. There was something'... more.

A darkness that latched itself onto me, waitin' to see how I'd react.

Maybe it's... A test, I rationalized. *It's time to show my faith.*

But how was I meant to do that while I was questioning every fiber of what made it true?

I rounded the corner, just barely catching the end of a long, dark ponytail disappearing around another bend up ahead.

Keeping my pace, it wasn't long until I rounded the corner myself, nearly bowlin' her clean over when I didn't spot her immediately in the low light. A terrified gasp escaped her as her eyes found mine behind her cornflower blue mask.

Ahead, the three others were carefully picking their way through the hall, avoiding certain parts of the floor. From a distance, I couldn't see what the problem was exactly, but there was only one answer that made sense.

Some kind of trap.

What the trap did didn't matter so much. Its existence was enough to delay progress.

At this point of the game, when the next heat of Runners

would be enterin' the arena at any moment, every second counted.

I continued to approach the girl, and she let out a terrified squeak, her eyes widening at the insignia on my bandana. There wasn't a doubt in my mind she'd clocked me as a Weston, her wide frightened eyes darting around my frame like by will alone she could change the cold, hard truth that I was the Ranch's top contestant this season.

But not the only one. The thought was bitter as bile on the back of my tongue.

My siblings had a bit of a different way of going about the Games, really taking the whole *make a show of it* thing count.

In Peter's Games, he'd waited until the end of the maze, his foot on a pressure plate that would collapse the rest of the corridor into a pit of lava. Burned the entirety of his alliance to ash in about twenty-five seconds.

He coulda disarmed it, coulda let the people that'd helped him get to that coveted finish line and cross it with him. But he'd decided to be cruel.

Bragged about it in his winner's interview.

Pa'd been beside himself with pride. Colored Peter with praise thicker than marmalade. I'd been *horrified*.

That was when I promised I wouldn't be like them.

When I realized that *for glory* didn't have to mean giving up your humanity.

I'd come to win, of course. But how I planned to do that was totally different from my kin before me. Where they were indiscriminate murderers with a penchant for high-profile, horrifyin' violence, I wanted to utilize my skills.

Wasn't enough to make it to the end because I'd taken the easy way out and mowed down anyone in my path. Naw, I wanted to cross that finish line—and cross it *first* because I'd trained. Because I was the best damn Runner to ever live. The product of decades of excellence.

A true Legacy.

"Don't come any closer!" Cornflower Blue shouted, taking a nervous step backwards into the hall.

"Aw, darlin'," I called, approaching slowly, my hands held out placatingly in front of me. A few more steps like that, and who knew what could happen. "I'm not going to hurt you, sugar, don't you worry now."

"God, you are so fucking full of it. You think you can just call me some pet names and I'll forget what you are? Fucking PK Weston *scum*!"

"I'm not my siblings," I reassured her, affronted. Maybe it was the bubble I lived in, but I'd never heard my family's methods questioned before. It was kind of... Excitin'. "I'm just here to play the game like you."

She backed up again as I neared, stumbling over her own feet and sprawling across the floor, her hand sinking slightly on a tile that'd depressed under her weight.

An alarm shrieked to life through the hallway as the lights changed, bathing us in red that all but blotted her features, that dark ponytail of her swaying with the shake of her head.

A low rumble turned into a roar as the tiles around her began to fall away, crumbling into darkness, her scream of terror swallowed by the onslaught of noise.

I jumped the gap formed by the initial few, grabbing the girl like a football while she tried to crab-crawl feebly away from the rapidly disappearing floor, hoisting her under one arm and running the length of the corridor full tilt.

The watch on my wrist buzzed, its face flashing red as I sprinted to safety. As if it wasn't already perfectly fuckin' clear that I was in the middle of a trap.

Game. Fuckin'. *On*.

Aubrey

I'm coming for you!

That useless fucking bitch wasn't just ahead of me.

She was *two heats* ahead of me.

I was agnostic at best—as if I'd let some fucking man tell me what I could and couldn't do. Especially one who only spoke to me through a book that was written thousands of years ago by—you guessed it—*men*! But if I did believe in God or a higher power or... *whatever*, I knew one thing and one thing only.

He had it out for me.

It was the only explanation for how the fuck this was happening to me again.

Sure, starting in fourth wasn't an immediate loss, but it was no secret that the sooner you got in, the better chance you had at getting to the end first. There were risks, at no point did you enter the maze without them, but the slightly increased chances of running headfirst into a trap didn't mean shit in comparison to a damn near half-hour head start. Besides, if you had half a brain, you could easily avoid them.

Just needed to be observant.

Basically, the same skills as searching for an actual staple piece at the outlet mall instead of last season's dime-a-dozen already out of fashion rejects.

Easy.

Only an idiot would think our positions were a coincidence. The Architects had planned who would go first as carefully as they had laid the traps to kill us. It was all for the good of the show.

For entertainment and wow factor—the Bachelorette for people with loose morals around killing. Who was I kidding? With the do-or-die attitude of some of those men? Same audience.

So why?

Why, why, why, why?

How the fuck *am I in lot* four?

I'd caught glimpses of the first heat as they stepped up onto the raised platforms, waiting for the catwalk to bridge the gap between them and the maze.

The fan favorites were unmissable—the last Ranch prodigy from the actual Weston line in the first group, no surprise there. But what was shocking? Hiram Wolff, a Legacy in his own right from his win decades ago in Hide N' Seek in heat *three*. Still waiting to even be allowed onto the platforms.

Even more shocking? I'd barely fucking noticed him, save for the way that everyone was giving him a wide berth like he had some sort of disease. I'd been too distracted by the Weston. My eyes caught on their wide shoulders, the cut-off sleeves of their black top only accentuating their muscular, heavily tattooed arms. The cowboy hat was a bit on the nose for my taste, but given I was dressed like Sailor Moon's slutty sister, I figured I should probably shut up.

But Hiram? That was worth noting, maybe even more than the veritable eye candy.

I'd *never* seen the Architects put one of their own in the ring, so whatever he'd done... it had to have been explosive.

Interesting.

I shuffled my feet, platform boots sinking slightly in the plasticized grass where I waited under a large banner that read *four*.

But Hiram's fall from grace wasn't the only thing pulling my attention around the room. There was something else that factored into Rat Race in a way that the other events lacked: *the live audience.*

In Hide N' Seek, the closest the watchers could get was through a phone screen—simply wouldn't do for a stray bullet to take out a paying customer, right? That left all the spectating to be done through large TVs and mobile phones. And Truth or Dare was too unpredictable in location for there to be a real studio audience factor. But this?

This was marketing gold.

The Company sold tickets at a premium, *obviously*, allowing our more affluent supporters the opportunity to glimpse us right before we went inside.

For some Runners—what they called the idiots who entered the maze—it would be the last time they'd be seen alive.

Idiots like me.

The semicircular stadium was filled to bursting. Watchers clutching popcorn and soft drinks alongside handmade signs for their favorite players. I spotted my name and face splashed across a few, some of my supporters even going so far as to have custom T-shirts, my own practiced smile staring back at me like a repeating mirror.

I searched the stands, finding my manager in the lower bowl beside the Mantene executives that'd signed off on my check. Sandy was a fucking cougar more interested in bagging her barely legal assistant than she was the success of her clients, but she was also cutthroat.

Ruthless.

The kind of woman that could get shit done.

Which made us a perfect match.

She pulled her bottle-copper hair around one side, flashing

her shoulder at me in an obvious order to move my hair off the back of my jacket.

I fought the urge to roll my eyes, complying with a fake-ass smile that earned me a thumbs up and a double-handed fake grab at her boobs with a smirk that I'd guessed meant she approved of my outfit.

Fucking perv. If I gave her half an inch, I knew she'd like nothing more than to be three acrylics deep in me.

As if.

Mine weren't the only sponsors to show up for their players, not to mention the holographic adverts that played while the countdown ran on the massive screen above, warning the next heat of players that their time to enter the maze was rapidly approaching.

I even caught myself on one of them. Smiling like it was my birthday before applying a thick layer of Purrfect Pout lip plumper.

To be fair, I actually liked the product—though nowhere near enough to front the sixty-five-dollar price point. Besides, it wasn't the lip plumper that gave me this signature pout. It was filler.

Duh.

The crowd was restless. Excited conversation and cheers turning into a welcome backing track as I waited for my chance to finally get my hands on the bitch. A task that'd be made more difficult by her sizable head start. But hey, I had always been good at catching up.

As it was, I didn't give two shits about the people behind me. As soon as I was placed in the large circle-shaped waiting area, my eyes sought her out.

It didn't matter that everyone had glowing masks. Or that many of the costumes were... *distracting*, to say the least. I found her almost immediately.

Natalie Phillips.

Turns out that after a lifetime of living in someone's shadow, you get pretty good at identifying them from behind. Especially after you factored in me chasing behind her as she raced ahead with her grubby little hands outstretched to grab ahold of literally *everything* I ever wanted.

Well, except cheer captain. Shout out to Vic for that one.

She was dressed in a light purple two-piece outfit that reminded me of our old cheer uniforms, warm brown hair styled in a lightly curled bouncy ponytail with a glittering bow. Her mask, a matching purple one with hearts for eyes, was sitting securely over her face.

I fought the urge to roll my eyes.

Could you be any more cliche?

Talk about peaked in fucking high school.

I'd imagined running up behind her and attacking her when she least expected it more times than I could count, if only to pass the time.

It was the least she deserved after the humiliation she put me through. After the *years* of coming in second.

Unacceptable.

My face burned just thinking about it.

There was only one thing that stopped me. Murder was illegal. It wouldn't bode well for an obvious front-runner such as myself to get banned from the Games before they even started.

I might not be a Legacy but I was as good as one—my mom worked in the Architects' office for most of my life. That meant status. Prestige.

Even if I did miss out on the media perks.

Just another way that cunt outshined me. The genetic fucking lottery.

But whatever, I just made sure to make my own. My beauty channel grew in subscribers every day. And four months after I turned eighteen and my after-dark channel went live, it exploded.

I mean, *obviously.*

The way I saw it, there wasn't much I could do in there to fuck this up aside from dying. Not a chance I'd lower myself back to the working class. No hate to the people who served me coffee

—they were providing the essential service of making sure I was caffeinated enough not to go to jail—but *fuck that*. I'd rather bleed out in the concrete death box, thanks.

It'd be downright embarrassing... and I couldn't take much more humiliation after what Natalie did.

I needed to redeem myself.

No, fuck that. I needed to eviscerate her.

It was just my luck she entered the Games because it totally solved all the pesky legalities associated with what I wanted to do to her.

The Games had rules, of course, what game didn't? But most of them had to do with the staff. The other players? They were free-range.

Fuck them.

Kill them.

Hell, you could probably resort to cannibalism if you could do it in a way that made people hand over their wallets.

The Architects didn't give a fuck as long as they were getting a good show out of it.

And if there was one thing I could do was give a satisfying performance.

I didn't care about the money. I had more than I needed from my family—*hello trust fund*—and sponsorships. Fuck, I didn't even care if I made it to the end at all.

There was only one goal that meant anything to me, as I watched her stupid high pony bouncing with her every movement.

I need to get to her.

As long as I could finally get my claws into Natalie, the rest would be worth it. Even if it did cost me my life. At least I'd be going out knowing that I'd gotten mine.

What? Was I just supposed to let some sleazebag stranger kill her? Or worse, her own stupidity when she inevitably fell into some trap?

That girl's blood belonged to me from the moment she dared step into my spotlight. And I was here to collect.

The timer reached the ten-second mark, the crowd beginning to chant the dwindling numbers as we were bathed in red light for a second time.

It seemed to go faster this time, the infectious energy of the crowd making my heart beat faster in my chest.

Once the light flipped to green, the catwalks snapping into place with a loud metallic click that was nearly drowned by the cheers and screams overhead, the Runners jerked into motion.

I watched with distaste as the girl who ruined my entire life was first in through the doors. The opening was large enough for me to see her turn to the left, but that was as far as I got.

No matter. I'd spent enough time chasing after her that I was confident I'd be able to think like her. I'd track her down in seconds, minutes if she was lucky.

The thought of cornering her in the maze had taken over my mind. Every waking minute since turning eighteen had been consumed by the fantasy of her death. It was rotting my mind, coating the surface like novocain. Making everything else duller by comparison.

It would be such sweet revenge. Not only would everyone watching see just how much better I was than her, but all those back home that dared look down on me would realize that I wasn't one to fuck around with. That they've made a horrible mistake.

Overhead, the screens changed, calling lot three to take the podiums as the catwalks moved back to the ground. The timer counted down, warning them their preparation period was quickly ending.

The screams I'd become accustomed to lowered to a murmur, the crowd whispering and jeering as Hiram took his podium. Even in his mask the man was obvious—the thing about Devil's Playground is there wasn't an age cap, not really. But it was, mostly, a young person's game.

Dude had to be pushing fucking fifty if the silvery hair poking out of the top of his mask was any indicator.

"Think he can feel the eyes on him?" A light, feminine voice asked from my left.

"Like being in the lion's den," I replied. There wasn't a single predator in this room that wouldn't be enticed by Vic's bounty.

Not to mention... free rein to kill an Architect? Even if he was disgraced there had to be a few Runners who would, well, *kill* for the chance. What a way to make a name for yourself.

Vic was a fucking genius. She could've let this play out with no interference; the likelihood of a man his age making it out of the maze was already statistically destitute. But to turn his own players against him?

To make the game he designed his prison?

I could fucking *come* from the cruelty of it.

Hiram's entire body was rigid, eyes scanning the crowd every few seconds like he really thought they'd kill him while he waited to be let into the maze.

A paranoid bastard if I ever saw one.

To be fair, maybe someone *would* take a swing on the way in. Vic wanted a laugh after all.

I could smell the stench of fear on him even from yards away. *Fucking pathetic.*

The timer hit zero, and lot three ran in there, desperation starting to show as Runners sprinted the length of the catwalk to disappear through the gates and into the maze.

I pushed forward with the crowd, breaking out to the front as the timer reset, waiting for my moment now.

"Aubrey! Aubrey! Aubrey!!!" I could hear my supporters chanting over the casual screaming now, earning a big smile and a wave as I turned on the spot, making sure to show off the logos on my jacket.

The clips of this moment would be all over every social media platform for the rest of my life, so I might as well take the time to play it up for the audience.

Electricity buzzed through the stadium. The remaining Runners with anxiety as their time drew closer. The watchers with excitement for the game to really begin.

Screams for favorite players. Curses for those they hated.

I *loved* it.

The seconds weighed on me, our waiting period feeling like hours instead of minutes. My heart pounded in my chest, blood rushing through my ears, making everything sound far away and tinny.

This was it.

My big opportunity.

All eyes were on the large interlocking doors as they opened, giving a sneak peek into the maze, even if it was only for a few feet. It was pitch black beyond the doorway, covered on all sides.

The only way out was through.

After the last lot, the doors would shut permanently, locking us in until we found our way to the other side or time ran out.

Well, unless we were being removed in a body bag. Not that I'd let that happen—black had never been my color.

As the numbers got smaller, I bent slightly at the knees, making sure to breathe deeply before I pushed off. My mind was in a flurry, thinking of every possible way I could run into her. How I would finally get the revenge that I craved so deeply.

If I was lucky, I'd find a weapon on the inside. But I wasn't above using my bare hands to choke the cunt to death if I had to.

I forced myself to quiet down, counting with the crowd, trying to match the numbers with my breathing.

My body tensed as my turn got closer and closer.

The crowd.

The players.

Everything faded into a sea of white noise, laser-focused into one thing and one thing only.

Her.

I'm coming for you.

The lights turned green, the audible click of the catwalk snapping into place barely registering. My body moved before my mind could catch up. Players all around me shouted as it was their turn to race toward the entrance. I wasn't there to race, but getting in the maze before the others would only help me get to her faster.

Adrenaline ran through me, pumping my legs faster than ever. I pushed past the wall of bodies, the anxiety in the air only making me that much more excited.

There were others stronger than me, who had more experience, were more vicious, but I was *faster*.

Despite how many were assigned to my gate, I was the first of my group to make it in, and I made an immediate left.

The temperature dropped five degrees as I entered the concrete-enclosed maze. Dim lights were spaced throughout, but they flickered in and out, causing gaps in my vision as I pushed my legs faster. The noise from the crowd and the players who were stuck fighting at the entrance faded into the background, leaving just me, the pounding of my platformed feet against the concrete floor, and my thoughts.

I'm late. She's probably already way ahead.

Frustration gnawed at me as I tried to orient myself. Turns out a completely enclosed maze was hard to navigate. No sun to give you any idea of the direction you were headed.

Just your intuition and a whole lot of hope.

Screams rang throughout the halls, echoing until they died down. The noise was coming from my right, and I took a sharp turn toward it.

I wasn't in it to save myself, and I didn't so much need the money. So the only logical option was for me to head straight into danger and just pray that I could get to her before one of the traps could.

The closer I got, the easier it was to make out the noise, the screams needing to hit fewer surfaces before they reached me. It wasn't just one. It was multiple.

Meaning there is a chance she's there too.

There was an empty rack as I took the next turn. I fought the urge to roll my eyes. If I'd been in an earlier lot, I probably would've been able to grab whatever had been on it—weapons, medical supplies, fuck, even a bottle of water would've been welcome. But that was the thing about being in lot four. I was just going to have to learn to make do.

I rounded the next turn, nearly stumbling over a body lying across the path, blood pooling beneath it in a puddle on the floor. The other players either hadn't tried to avoid it or hadn't been able to, leaving a trail of sticky, crimson footsteps on the concrete.

A pair of Runners were fighting in the distance, their masks glowing yellow and green in the dim light. It was hard to tell who had the upper hand, the pair clashing violently with their fists.

A bit barbaric, really. But I didn't have time to worry about that, not with disappointment clawing at my throat like when I'd lost out on Homecoming Queen.

Natalie wasn't here.

I cursed under my breath.

Another left, maybe?

Just as I was about to move on from the fighting pair, movement further down the hall caught my eye. My spirits lifted immediately at my good luck.

Hello, cunt.

She was down at the end of the hallway, watching it all. Of course that cunt had her nose in everyone's business.

A smile twisted my face, and a crazed chuckle passed my lips.

Got you.

I charged forward and right into the fighting men with my shoulder, the force of my body colliding with them knocking them to the ground. Their surprised shout rang through the hallway, smearing some of the blood from their brawl across my arms as they tried to grab me.

One got a hold of my jacket, but I slipped out of the heavy material with ease. Nothing was going to keep me from my goal. Not even a fucking contract.

Curses followed me as I ran after the girl.

"Hey!"

"Fucking bitch!"

But their shouts returned to grunts and sickening blows of flesh against flesh as one of them used my distraction to get an upper hand on the other. I didn't have to look back to know that one of them was probably sinking a blade into the other's chest. The grunts and pained gurgling told me all I needed to know.

Which meant I needed to get the fuck out of here and fast. Deal with my little problem and get as much distance between me and an armed man twice my size as quickly as possible.

Natalie hadn't expected me to come right at her, something that was made obvious by the panicked noise she released when her singular brain cell worked out that I was barreling toward her. She turned on her heel, sprinting for the end of the hall and then hastily turning to the right.

I was right behind her, almost enough to touch. I took my chance, reaching my hand out in an attempt to grab her. Her long, flowy locks brushed my fingertips, but it wasn't enough to hold on, the end of her dark ponytail slipping through my fingers like water.

Like every opportunity she'd ever stolen from me.

So close.

So close I could taste the sweetness of revenge on my tongue, not to be confused with her cheap, overly vanilla perfume. And it'd been so easy.

We passed another opening, and not one, but three people were rushing down the hallway toward us and away from something. I skidded to a halt in order not to crash right into them.

It was all the time Natalie needed to disappear from my line of vision, dipping around a corner.

Fuck, are you kidding me?

A hard body slamming into mine knocked me off balance and sent me sprawling. Pain shot up my back as my ass came into contact with the hard floor.

They were running from something. Was it this person?

I raised my shaking hand on instinct.

"Please!" I forced out in a high-pitched whine, the second part of my strategy for the maze coming into play sooner than I would've liked as I kept my eyes screwed tightly shut, braced for impact. "Please don't hurt me, I just want to get out of here!"

But the blow I was waiting for never came. Heavy panting reached my ears, the seconds ticking by making me curious. I peeled my eyes open to come face to face with... *Hiram.* He was breathing heavily, a broken-off spike in one of his clenched fists.

Where the hell did he get a weapon already?

But if they were running from him... I could use this.

"Please," I whimpered and pushed myself to my knees, clutching at his clothes desperately. "Don't hurt me! We can help each other!"

"Help each other?" he said, tilting his head to the side as he stepped out of my hold. He was still breathing heavily from the chase, obviously not used to this type of workout.

Turns out a couple decades in the Architect's office wasn't so good for your cardio. Good. It meant that, if I needed to, I'd be able to get away from him.

Or maybe I'd turn on him myself—claim Vic's money. Either way, I could decide later; for now, I needed to convince him not to kill me. And to prioritize going after Natalie.

I nodded quickly. "For traps, you know?" I explained and inched toward him on my knees on the hard floor, my hands out, palms facing him. "Please? I'm *begging*. I'll help you any way I can, be loyal only to *you.*"

His eyes shifted to the side as the sound of footsteps reached us. Not just one, but multiple people were likely on our trail—he had a choice to make, and quickly.

Either the weak, innocent young girl promising him loyalty for a bit of his help or other players that likely wanted him for the bounty.

There was a heavy pause, Hiram's dark eyes meeting mine before he gave a sharp nod.

"I want to get out of here in record time, okay?" he said and motioned for me to follow him. I had to hope he picked the same path as Natalie, though, without seeing where she went myself, his guess was as good as mine.

"Yes, sir," I replied and forced myself to my feet, trotting obediently along after him, trying and failing to keep the smile off my face.

Cam

"Would you put me the fuck down?" the ragdoll snapped, hair swayin' as I whipped around corners.

Our watches had gone green a while ago, but I was still eager to get some space between us and the first trap—as well as any of the other Runners that'd be coming up close behind us.

In all honesty, I'd have forgotten the girl was there if it wasn't for her bitchin' and moanin'. Even if she was wrigglin' like a fuckin' piglet.

You'd think she'd be at least a tiny bit grateful that I'd saved her life, but given the attitude? That dog wouldn't be huntin' any time soon.

Fuckin' civilians. I'd never understand why they let people with no training sign up for this thing. Call it being old-fashioned, but I just thought that everyone deserved the opportunity to learn how to identify a pressure plate before throwing them into the maze.

I picked down the next hallway carefully—a task made more difficult as the blue-masked girl in my arms continued to fight to get free.

"Naw, sugar. I reckon you're no good at traps like this," I said, glancing at the light on my watch, a yellow light cheerily now reminding me that we weren't clear of danger. There had to be another trap close by. "Lemme take care of this for ya. Be a shame not to make it to stage two, right?"

The maze was divided into two distinct stages, usually split down the middle by an *oasis*, a zone of play generally agreed upon by the Runners to be a no PK zone—y'know, no murderin' each other. It acted as a rest stop in the middle of the most physically demanding of the Games. A place to refuel and prepare for the fresh horrors lyin' in wait ahead.

I half hoped I'd see Elijah there. As much as I sort of hoped he was already dead.

Fuck, I really needed to get my head on straight.

"Put me down, you big, stupid, fucking—" the girl shouted, making me wince at the proximity to my ear.

I wrinkled my nose. "Hey now, don't get ugly with me. I'm saving your life! Coulda let you wander off over yonder and to your death ages ago, so least you can do is say *thank you* and talk at a fuckin' reasonable volume."

Y'know, city folk always looked down on people like me with my so-called simple accent and lack of big-name university degree —and fuckin' sue me if boots and jeans felt more comfortable than pencil skirts and stilettos. Though, even if I were one of them sophisticated city types, I reckoned I'd be more interested in suits.

Dresses weren't really my thing, at least not the ones Ma and my sisters wore. Frilly little things edged with lace in Easter colors. Usually with a matching hat that looked more like a frisbee than headwear.

A flash of green on my wristlet, paired with a thumbs-up emoji, warned that we'd made it through the kill zone, and I, rather hastily, dumped my ungrateful tagalong onto the ground.

My thick arms crossed as she scrambled up from the dirty floor to meet my raised eyebrow with her furious glower like a cat fresh outta the bath.

"You could've put me down nicely!"

I also coulda left ya there to die. But I didn't say that. Instead, I went the more polite route. The Ranch wasn't just good for teaching us murderin'. Manners were important too.

"Coulda," I agreed. "But given I saved your life just now and I've yet to hear a *thank you*, figured that fair was fair. Well, good luck, miss," I said, tipping my hat to her and turning to continue my path up the hall with a glance at my watch.

> B1GGYB0Y
>
> Good riddance!!
>
> ELLEMAEBOOKS
>
> WESTONS 4EVER!!!
>
> AUTHORBEXDEVEAU
>
> Keeping it CUNTry!

There was a pause, the only sounds her panicky, shallow breathing and my boots against the concrete while she seemed to wrestle with the idea that she'd nearly died back there.

Civvies. I tell ya, reckon they can just sign up and win, no forethought. No plan.

Never mind the fact Billy'd trained from birth for this thing and still didn't manage to make it out.

You could kill her, a voice whispered in the back of my mind. An unfamiliar dark corner that wriggled just out of reach. *Make a show of it.*

Given Blue's performance so far, I'd made a snap assessment that she wasn't a Legacy. Most of us had some kind of background knowledge of how the traps worked. It was one of the perks of having winner parents—even if those winners weren't the militant training organization that was the Ranch, they could at least offer you a little advice.

If she kept at it like this, it would be her funeral, *literally*.

Clumsy girls were usually better at Hide N' Seek. Rat Race was too much on the athletic side—like a real sport, only every time you played it you had an above-average chance of meetin' the good Lord instead of headin' home with a participation ribbon.

But death was what made it entertainin' to the millions of people watching at home. It's what paved the way for my family's career. Hell, paid *lots* of people *lots* of money. The impact of the Games alone had been the biggest economic boost in the entire century.

Like the Olympics, but annually. A massive amount of ad spend, hospitality dollars, and good old-fashioned taxes on bettin' wins.

And that was only the aboveboard shit.

No matter how wholly fucked the idea of watchin' people kill themselves for a couple trophies and a bit of money was, there was no puttin' a stop to it. Thousands of people could die—had—died. But that didn't change a thing. Population control. Natural selection. Just the cost of doin' business. Whatever you wanted to call it, I reckoned that as long as Devil's Playground kept lining the pockets of the right politicians, it'd never be stopped.

Do you get mad at the farmers for raising the pigs or at the people eating the bacon?

It was circle of life shit, and I wasn't gonna change it.

Naw, I'm here to win the whole damn thing, right?

Give 'em a good show, make the Ranch some money, bring honor to my parents, and get myself the fuck outta here.

Yes, Lord.

I took a deep breath, slowing my racing heart. Even after years of training, I still found the maze... disorienting. Especially carryin' my extra baggage.

There's no way she'll make it if she doesn't tag along.

Which means I'd be forced to take her.

For once, I almost wished that I was like my cruel siblings. It'd be way easier to leave her here to die, givin' me a higher chance at winning if I wasn't slowed down by someone with no training.

But I couldn't do it and still live with myself after.

Fuckin' cock on a rock.

Just ahead was a T in the path, a flat wall that ended in a dead end, forcing us to choose a direction. Historically, the finish line was in a central position, but that didn't mean cow shit to me. In here, history books were best used as a blunt weapon to try and kill a stray rat.

It was all about instinct and hints. I looked at my watch, but the comments from my viewers weren't helpful—not that they could be if I was in the lead. Means they wouldn't've seen nobody come to this location yet. Not that it mattered too much, but my gut was saying that the left was the way to go.

Usually, it was worth listenin' too.

I was just looking down the hall when the girl's voice made me pause.

"Where are you going?" she asked. Hesitant, maybe even a little scared.

Tug at the heartstrings, why don't ya?

"O'er yonder to the finish line, sugar," I answered, hooking my thumb toward the left path. "You gonna sit there like a bump on a log or come along?"

She slowly got to her feet, taking a few careful steps toward me.

"You're really not a PKer?"

"Naw, blood makes me squeamish." An outright lie. I'd grown up on the Ranch for fuck's sake, but it made her shoulders relax nonetheless.

Never you mind that I coulda split her head open easier than peeling an orange.

She really shouldn't be so trustin'. You never knew who you were spendin' time with down here.

"Okay... I... uh... I'm Ella. T-Thank you. For not letting me fall."

"Cam," I replied with a nod. "Don't worry about it too much —gratitude does go a long way though," I said, flashing a cheeky smile and turning to motion for her to follow. "C'mon, we need to get movin'. Slow and steady doesn't do fuck all in here."

"Cam," Ella repeated thoughtfully, jogging to catch up so our arms brushed as we walked along the left-hand corridor. "Oh--- *Camilla*. I should have recognized which Weston you were"

"The one and only. See, I'm not tryin' to hurt ya. No PKs in my pre-game stats, right?"

"Strategies change," Ella hedged, tightening her ponytail. Her eyes were searching my masked face as if it would tell her whether I was lyin'.

I couldn't tell behind the blue glow of hers if she was scowlin' or not, but I guessed so from her general air of displeasure.

"Sure," I agreed, scratching thoughtfully at some of the tattoos covering my throat. "But I tend to be pretty set on not murderin' nobody. I take it you aren't a Legacy then?"

Ella's laugh was the sort that made it clear she didn't find my question funny, which it wasn't meant to be in the first place. There was a tinge of hysteria to it, like she wasn't quite right. Though, I guessed if you were willing to sign yourself up for this shit, there had to be somethin' fuckin' wrong with you.

Ma and Pa made it crystal clear that I was either to be one in a long line of success stories or they'd let my body rot outside in the Texas heat after Devil's Playground delivered it. Not exactly the warm, nurturing types you expected of typical southern families.

To be fair, fuck all about us was typical. Our family ranch went from raising cattle to... Well, I guess technically we still raised cattle. In the sense that they raised children—their own and other people's—for the sole purpose of being able to enter them into the Games.

We raised prizewinning pigs.

Legends.

Legacies.

The type of people that could change the entire fabric of their family tree—if you had the money. Which we did. Back in our long family history, we'd been nothing but poor farmers. The same farm we lived on now had been passed down for generations before the Games even started.

They would never guess how the family changed. **What** *we changed into.*

Monsters dressed as fuckin' ministers. Though I reckoned a lotta churches had those.

"No," Ella said finally. "I'm not a Legacy. I grew up on a hobby farm with artists for parents. My mom is—was—a potter."

"Like cups and bowls and stuff?" I asked, stopping off to grab a couple bottles of water from a recession in the wall and handing one to her.

She nodded, muttering a quick *thank you.* "Yeah. My dad was an accountant. But his real love was like, farming? Probably seems a bit silly to you, I guess."

"Naw," I said, cracking the top of my bottle and pushing my mask up for a long drink. "It's sorta nice, normal. Crops or animals?"

"Both. Horses, goats, a couple cows. I even grew up with pet chickens. Got one now—Amelia Egghart."

I laughed, a sudden tug of warmth for the brunette enough for me to know I'd made the right call.

"Mine was Hennifer."

"And how was Hennifer's body?" Ella asked, the smile evident in her voice even before she was pushing her mask up to drink her water.

"Delicious."

Fine, maybe I cared just a little that Amelia Egghart would be an orphan or whatever. It was stupid, but it didn't change how I felt.

We shared a fond glance, the connection from back home solidifying our alliance.

The scent of rain was heavy the closer we got to the next bend, the metal pipes overhead pumping in fresh air from the surface. I sniffed hard, listenin' in the eerie quiet for the sound of the mechanisms that'd warn of an oncoming attack.

Rain? Did it start raining after the other lots entered?

There was no telltale ping to warn about new dangers, just the running stream of feedback from viewers. I glanced around, flashing a little wink at one of the cameras.

We took a left, then were forced to the right, the path ahead opening up into a square room. The far wall was smooth except for a seam in its middle, the rest of the room with ends of dozens of pipes poking from the rock.

Overhead, the Devil's Playground theme crackled lightly through the speakers as we entered. Slowly, I walked around the perimeter, looking for loose bricks, pressure plates, rope... a big red shining button? Anything that would offer a hint about how we were supposed to get the doors to open.

The watch on my wrist buzzed, the feed of chatter suggestions moving too fast for me to make sense of it beyond the idea that maybe the pipes overhead had something to do with the solution. But that seemed a bit... overly simplistic for the maze.

I'd just opened my mouth to ask Ella what she thought when colored ropes descended from the ceiling at different lengths, their ends hidden by holes that could be several inches or feet deep.

"Dead end?" Ella said, huffing with irritation. "That's going to really slow us down... Fuck, we needed to move faster."

"Naw, not a dead end." I corrected her, motioning to the seam in the wall. "Look."

It felt a bit like counsellin' the younger kids on how to solve the puzzles inside the maze. Obvious to me but lost on them.

"C'mon now, you're smart as a whip. You gotta be able to see it, right?"

"A big flat wall, yeah, I see it, genius." She sighed, looking around the rest of the room. "Those holes aren't big enough for us to fit through," she added, her hand stretching out to wrap her fingers around one of the ropes.

I fought the urge to roll my eyes, forcibly taking her chin in my hand to turn her head to look at the seam. "Naw, sugar, one of those must open *that*. Not a fuckin' clue how we're supposed to know which one, though."

"Right," she mumbled, shaking my hand off and staggering back.

It was almost cute how clueless she was. At least I reckoned it would've been if she wasn't a total disaster who was gonna get us both killed.

I didn't have time to play no fuckin' babysitter. I was here to win, by any means necessary.

"Well," Ella said, fingers tightening on the rope. "I guess we just try one?"

"Hello!" A cheery, masculine voice called over the intercom system. "The Company is happy to provide you some assistance in the form of a riddle clue—"

Ella yanked on the nearest rope, a low rumbling beginning in the distance. A bit like the sound of a lot of pressure being released all at once. My lips parted as I looked first at the seam in the door and then at the intercom, my heart already beginning to race.

Couldn't be fuckin' good.

The cheery male voice had a definitive air of irritation as it came through the speaker again. "Well, I did have a whole thing planned. Was sort of my one job to read these to you, but since you decided to be a dick and not listen, I'll have to give you a different one."

Ella tried to shove the door open with brute force, her shoulder hitting the rock as if it were made of steel. Surprising absolutely no one, she fell backwards. The doors didn't even have the good manners to quiver.

"I'm sorry, mister!" I shouted up at the speaker as Ella tried to pry the gap open with her hands. "Ella! Quit that and come apologize for Christ's sake. The nice fella is going to get us a clue."

Overhead the pipes groaned, the wind roaring miles above making Ella jump.

"Okay, okay!" Ella said, her terrified eyes flicking to mine. "I'm sorry! What are the clues?!"

There was a sigh, the masculine voice clearly irritated that his perfect setup had been interrupted. "Oh, so we *are* going to play? Fine. Look down, look down. Stop at the stone that makes a sound."

"Stone that makes a sound?" I muttered, crouching to take in the stone floor for anythin' that might've been invisible to the naked eye in the low light. I'd been so busy looking for pressure plates that I hadn't been botherin' to take notice of anything else. "Ella, walk the length of the room, and listen for a loose tile." I ordered, doing the same on the other side.

It took a few passes before I found it, close to the middle, a tile that, when stepped on, let out a metallic sort of clang. I bent, my fingertips moving along the ridges until they caught on an uneven bit at the tile's edge, yanking it up to reveal the start of what looked like a trap door.

"Ella! Come help me, would ya?" I called to the brunette, grunting slightly as I pulled up tile after tile.

The group of them seemed to interlock on a tongue-and-groove system like puzzle pieces, lifting away easily after the first was pulled. Ella came to join me, pulling more until a six-foot square was uncovered, large silvery metal rings screwed into the surface of a painted black surface.

"Grab one," I ordered unceremoniously, taking hold of the other with both hands. She followed my instructions, and I braced myself, preparin' to do the lion's share of the work. "Pull."

I yanked on the ring, surprised when the wood didn't fall away and pulled upwards instead, a stone box standing at table height when all was said and done. A mechanical click let us know that the box was secured in place.

It was like some sort of altar—fitting, since I reckoned I was in the middle of yet another test.

Make a show of it.

There was a small latch on the side that I opened, revealing a sliding puzzle underneath the hinged lid of the table.

My watch and Ella's blared to life, the screens lightin' crimson as our startled eyes met each other.

"Timer," Ella supplied, lookin' uneasily around at the pipes. "Could be gas, or water, or... or—"

"Ella, focus," I told her softly. Then, raisin' my voice a bit to the speaker box, I added, "Don't suppose you got some advice?"

"Above my pay grade," the masculine voice called.

Lord have mercy.

I turned back to the table, studyin' the pieces and tryin' to make sense of what the image could be. Waves of brightly colored somethin'. Red and white stripes. Mechanical parts that looked like they could be...

I didn't know.

Familiar and foreign all at the same time.

Fuck me, I was no good at shit like this.

"It's a postcard," Ella said, her eyes movin' over the table like lightnin'. "At least... I think so. See this here? It's the stamp, right?"

"I—" I started, tracking her finger to the image of the flag, the white scalloped edges around it.

Okay, yeah... It was a postcard, maybe... But, of what?

I looked over the colors and shapes again, pickin' out pieces of letters, the machinery starting to look more n' more like... rides.

She placed her hand on one of the pieces closest to the empty space, sliding it to the left.

A trickle of water had begun to drip from overhead, steadily increasing with every movement of the blocks.

"I don't see how this will tell us what rope to pick," she said, frowning as she continued to work the puzzle.

"Well," snarked the voice over the intercom. "If you'd listened first, I might've explained that getting the riddles right would drop the incorrect options. Make it easier."

"Woulda," I repeated with a little chuckle. "Sorry. Ella here has a fuckin' bee in her bonnet."

There was no reply from above, but Ella muttered under her breath. "I just want out of here."

Kill her, Pa's voice commanded. *She's already slowed you down.*

I pushed the thought away, watchin' as she slid the pieces around the table quickly, the picture of the Devil's Playground theme park slowly startin' to take form as she worked through the puzzle.

Feelin' a bit like a bump on a log, I hunted around for somethin' to say. Finally settlin' on, "So if you aren't a Legacy, why enter?"

"Why does anyone enter?" Ella hedged, her movements becoming rougher, shoulders high and tight.

Okay, touchy subject.

"Money, usually," I conceded, lookin' down at a tickle on my arm to find a cockroach crawlin' up from my hand. I brushed the bug away with a frown, lookin' up from the puzzle for the first time in several minutes and blinking in surprise.

Hundreds of the bugs—big enough that they'd need to get on their knees to fuck a chicken—covered the room from floor to ceiling, pourin' from the pipes overhead. Gross, but not exactly a cause for concern.

Ella didn't agree, her bloodcurdling scream bouncing off the walls as she climbed onto the table, shakin' one of the bugs out of her hair. Not that it did her any fuckin' good. The big bastards were everywhere, their hideous little bodies racing for the corridor we'd entered through where they appeared to congregate, crawling up the clear gap as easily as if it were a flat surface.

Fuck.

We were boxed in. And I was too damn stupid to notice.

"Get off the fuckin' table, Ella. We need to figure out the question."

"No! Oh my God! Oh my God! Cam, they're *everywhere*!" She screamed again, and I covered my ears, irritation lickin' up my spine. I couldn't stand screechin'. "Water!"

Maybe it would be easier to just make a show of it and get it over with already.

But I didn't want to be like that. Like *them*.

"Christ on a cracker," I hissed, shoving the girl off the table to continue workin' the puzzle. With every move of the blocks, the water seemed to increase in pressure.

Fuck fuck fuck fuck fuck.

It wasn't timed! It had a maximum number of moves. And if I had to guess, we were quickly approachin' the limit.

Goddamn it.

I looked at the pieces of words, tryin' to guess what the rest of the question could be with the ones left. Made more difficult with Ella blockin' half the pieces.

Really, I needed her to try and finish this fuckin' thing. I was dead awful at puzzles, and if every wrong move I made fucked it more... But Ella was too busy trying to rid herself of an ample coating of bugs to be any help.

For a second, I considered if I'd really be better off leavin' her behind. She was slow, frightened, and easily sent into a panic, not to mention clumsy. I needed an ally that could be an asset. Not another fuckin' drawback.

But that wasn't who I *wanted* to be. The Ranch might've taught me to *think* like them, but it was up to me if I wanted to *act* like them.

Westons? They used and abused people like they were animals bred for slaughter.

I wanted to be *different*.

Fair.

To treat people with respect. Be compassionate and all that other bullshit city folk nonsense. I didn't want to become like them. I wouldn't allow myself to.

I'd changed. Grown.

Grabbing her arm, I yanked the girl off the table and to her feet as the water began to form a deep puddle in the center of the room, forcing the wildlife closer to the doorway.

"Can you please, for five minutes, act like we are in the middle of somethin' bigger than a room full of critters? The clue, Ella. What's the fuckin' answer, sugar?"

She hesitated, her breath comin' in wild pants as her eyes darted around the room. I'd seen looks like this before. Usually after finding a horse without a rider on the trails on the back end of the Ranch's property. Spooked after seein' a rattler or somethin'. Dumped their rider further up the creek and took off.

As the moments ticked by, and the water continued to rise, the puddle growing until the water was sloshing at our ankles and lapping along the walls of the room, my patience thinned.

"Sugar," I repeated, tryin' to empathize with her fear. But if the girl didn't get a fuckin' grip and stop moaning, I was pretty damn sure we were gonna drown in a sea of filthy fuckin' roach water. "Please?"

Ma wouldn't even bother hostin' my wake.

Kill her. Kill her. Kill her.

I squeezed my eyes shut, trying to quiet the roar of water and unpleasant demands in my ears. I'd realized my mistake a second too late, with Ella's rushing footsteps splashin' as she raced for the wall of ropes. I tried to make a grab for her, but I was too slow, her hands closing around two ropes as she pulled down hard.

"You shouldn't have done that," the voice sighed over the intercom, the seam in the wall opening with a roar of water. "Who's out of time, has to say goodbye, and never getting out alive?"

Didn't have to be no fuckin' genius to work that one out.

Us.

A robotic buzzer noise sounded like we'd lost a low stakes carnival game. The dim lights of the room shifted red, a loud siren beginning to blare, making it hard to think. The pipes exploded into waterfalls, the puddle lapping at our ankles rising to our knees in seconds.

Ella tried to run the way we'd come, her little fists banging on the invisible barrier that the roaches were still trying to crawl up— the ones that weren't floatin' around us in the water at least.

I didn't have time to think. Picking up one of the heavy blocks from the puzzle table, I took a few steps, slowed by the water, now up to my thighs.

"Move it, sugar!"

She turned, duckin' out of the way just in time for me to miss her with the brick. But it just bounced off the barrier and flung itself back at us.

Fuck. Fuck. Fuck. Fuck. Fuck.

Okay, Cam. Think. Look. Deep breaths. Do not spin out.

My eyes moved around the room desperately, looking for somethin'—anythin'—to help us out of this mess when my eyes caught on a tiny gap where bugs were disappearing beside the barrier.

The water was already to my chest by the time I made it to the wall, usin' my fingertips to pry the hidden panel open to a swarm of writhing bodies covering an electric panel.

Doin' my best to dry my hand, I took a deep breath, throwin' my fist into the machinery. Punchin' and punchin' until my knuckles split open and the siren stopped with a peel of feedback.

I grabbed the back of Ella's shirt to stop her nearly overbalancin' as the current of water tried to pull her down, free to run now that the barrier had fallen.

But instead of starting to thin, the roar became louder.

I cursed, yanking her behind me as I began to run, trying to get ahead of the Architects' renewed efforts to drown us in the form of a giant wave rocketing from the door and pipes.

"Run!"

Aubrey

Not the fucking time to be simping.

He's not very talkative.

And, as far as I could tell, he didn't trust me very much, but that was neither here nor there.

At the very least, Hiram had believed my act enough that he was willing to underestimate me. Keeping me behind him as we walked, my eyes on his back and gray hair. But it wasn't enough to ignore me completely. Every few steps he'd turn his head and look to check I was still there.

Or maybe it was to make sure I didn't have a weapon pointed at his back.

None of my business, really. It was in his best interest not to trust me. It was in mine to make him forget that.

"I'm scared," I muttered softly, sniffing a little in the underground chill of the maze.

Dark, damp, and dirty. This place was a far cry from the modern metallic Tron-inspired arena of a few years ago.

It was always a bummer when they decided to go rustic. I was really hoping for more of a high-tech feel. It would be less... icky.

I fucking *hated* dirt. But more than dirt, I hated being bored.

And the long walk through dusty, half-moldy, rocky hallways

was more than a little boring. So boring that I was tempted to mess with Hiram a little just to fill the time.

Maybe set off a trap? That'd kill some time.

But the more time I killed, the further I was from realizing my dream of slicing open Natalie's throat like a fucking juice pouch.

"Are you sure we're going the right way?" I asked, adding a heavy dose of doe-eyed innocence. "We haven't run into anyone in a long ti—"

"I know what I'm doing," Hiram said with a huff, looking back at me in his glowing yellow mask with an irritated shake of his head. "I was an Architect, you know. I have this place memorized."

A man can't help but brag. At least I didn't have to hide the sly smile that appeared behind the mask. A little fluffing of his ego, and surely I'd be on my way to earning a bit of trust in no time.

"Wow, *really?*" I asked, skipping up to his side with an excited little jump. "That's so cool!"

Hiram jerked to the side, his entire body flinching as if he expected me to chop him down right then and there. I could just make out a bit of his face behind the mask from my angle, but it gave me no indication of how he was feeling. Based on his body language, I assumed he was frowning under there.

He upped our pace, and I fell beside him easily.

If that's how you want it.

If the man felt better with me at his back, I wouldn't crush his ego so soon. But as an Architect, he should know the most dangerous place for me to be was at his back, not at his side.

He gave me a side-long look before letting out a huff.

"It *was,*" he muttered under his breath. "I had everything. I was the best. They're fucking stupid for making me—"

His voice turned to background noise as soon as I saw *her.* Or at least her hair.

She was hiding around the corner, probably not expecting us to cover so much ground in such a short time.

Is she waiting for us? Maybe even attempting to follow us once we gain enough ground?

It was just like her. Using other people's talents and hard work and swooping in to take the credit for herself.

But not this time. This time, I caught her first.

A sick, excited feeling sprouted in my chest and sent butterflies scattering throughout my stomach.

Not so impressive now, huh? How will it feel for everyone to find out what a fucking fraud you are before your death?

I had my suspicions since it was almost impossible for her to have always been ahead of me. Seeing her in the maze just proved me right. Maybe instead of being one step ahead of me, she was actually just around the corner, spying and biding her time so she could jump ahead.

"This way!" I whispered excitedly to Hiram.

I didn't bother to look back and see if he was following me as I took off after her. His footsteps behind me were evidence enough that I had caught his attention.

Him following me didn't matter much, but what did was that I would have a way out after I finished her.

As soon as I rounded the corner, I regretted it.

"Wait!"

But Hiram's voice was drowned out by the sound of her scream and the rushing sound of something metallic clanking against the stone beneath our feet.

My eyes widened as I took in the dark hallway. I could make out her shape as she ran toward us along in her glowing yellow mask. What I thought were shadows behind her, were actually moving. Getting closer and closer as she ran.

That's when I saw the glowing red eyes.

She zoomed past me only to turn around and pause when she saw Hiram coming up to my side.

Bulls. There were ten—no, *more*—mechanical bulls heading right toward us. All of them charging at full speed with no indication that they would be stopping anytime soon.

But that didn't matter to her. Not when by my side was the world's most valuable Architect.

"You're the one with the bounty," she said, her voice sounding slightly crazed. She took a step toward him, her hands lashing out wildly to grab onto his shirt. "A million dollars."

This is my chance.

Hiram jerked out of her reach and right into me as I reached for her. I didn't care about the bulls behind us, their iron hooves echoing throughout the small space, sounding more like thunder than hooves. They rattled my brain, drowning out the shrill of the scream I knew I should have heard.

I didn't care that he was pushing me.

I didn't care that if I had lingered like I wanted to, I would have been dead.

All I cared about was *her*.

I could see the ending in my mind. Her on the ground, her head bashed open. I would watch as she took her last few breaths of air, and she would be watching me as I towered over her.

It would be quick but effective. A sight I would never get out of my head for as long as I lived.

I wondered what her last thoughts would be. If she would be sorry about the way she treated me or if, up until the very end, she would still think she was better than me.

I hope she cursed my name as she felt her pitiful life slip from those ugly, fucked-up nails of hers.

*I mean, how many times can someone get **that** shade of vomit green?*

An exhilarating thrill ran through me. This is the end. Not only was I going to see it, but I was going to be the one to usher her to it.

But there was one thing I didn't plan for.

I had researched other mazes. Watched hundreds of hours of replays. Fuck, I had even started paying more attention to the cunt just so I had a better idea of how she might act in the maze.

But I hadn't prepped for a certain, annoying Architect who

was so hell-bent on saving his miniscule life that he would ruin mine.

I had accidentally put myself right in the middle of Hiram's safety. I doubted he had any thought to save me—that would be out of character for him. He was probably hoping a trap would get me at some point. But he pushed us both out of the way in an attempt to get to the other side of the hallway.

And as she was moving toward him, her eyes still wide, he was the one to grab her first and use her body as the propellent he needed to get to safety.

I couldn't fully understand it as it happened. I took in every detail. Every sight. Every sound.

Yet I couldn't wrap my head around how on earth one minute she was there in front of me and the next, her body was being crushed under the bulls' hooves as they turned around the curb and down the hallway we had originally come from.

That's not right.

It was supposed to be me. Me. ME.

My mind was screaming at me to move. To do something. To fix this utterly disgusting wrong.

But I couldn't.

"Move, damn it!" he growled and pushed us further down the hallway. "The bulls are programmed on a certain route. If you don't move your ass, I'll lose a fucking foot!"

It was supposed to be me. Me. Me. Me.

He didn't even blink at what he did. *He* pushed her in front of the bulls. All because she wanted the bounty he had on his head.

Like she was nothing.

Which she was, but how long had I been waiting for my opportunity? How long had I been dreaming about the day when I would finally be able to make the bitch pay for what she'd done?

And now she's dead. I was supposed to kill her. ME.

No fanfare. No begging. Nothing to show the cameras. Nothing to watch back.

I wasn't even the one to push her, for fuck's sake.

I stood still, unable to move, until the bulls left and I finally saw what was left of her body.

It was an insult. A FUCKING INSULT. She was hardly even recognizable. The pretty image I had of her in my version of her death was far better than the real-life version. The real-life version was just... bland.

Especially when it was this bastard who dealt the final blow.

"You killed her," I muttered, my voice empty.

"She was trying to kill me! Us!" he corrected, his voice rising. "If I hadn't moved us out of the way—"

"You *killed* her," I muttered again. I spotted the spike he had been holding onto on the ground. My mind had never been clearer. My goal never this concrete.

The screaming in my head quieted for a moment and was replaced with a whisper.

You know what you need to do.

Quicker than he could stop me, I leaned down and picked it up only to point it right at him.

"Sorry, was that your friend or something? You didn't say anything—"

"A friend?" I asked with a crazed laugh. "You think *she* was my *friend?*" My voice kept rising with each word. "We were not *fucking friends!*"

I inched closer and closer, backing him into a wall before he held his hands up, real fear crossing his face.

"Okay, okay, I did—"

"She was *mine*," I said in a low growl, placing the spike right over his heart. "She was mine, you dipshit, and you took everything I wanted from me."

He swallowed thickly. "Look, I didn't know. I can still get us out of here—"

I threw my head back, my laugh echoing through the halls.

"You think I fucking care about getting out of here?" I asked. "You think I followed you because I wanted to get out of here? I wanted *her* end of story. And you took that from me. How would you ever be able to repay me?"

This time he didn't even try to open his mouth and talk his way out of this one.

"A life for a life," I whispered and pushed the sharp metal into his chest. It would take some work to push the spike into the wall of his chest cavity, but I was nothing if not an optimist.

Fury blinded me, but it wasn't enough for me to ignore the sudden noise of hundreds of tiny feet hitting the stone.

What the—

We both turned down the hallway to see hundreds of rats coming toward us. There was something rumbling in the background.

Another trap?

I expected another set of bulls to come running down the hallway, but instead, I saw the Weston prodigy, their large tattooed arms and cowboy hat calling attention to them right away. Their red mask was like a beacon as they ran full speed in our direction. They were the type to enter the Games and fucking dominate. Clear a path and force themselves out as first without even breaking a sweat.

Their arms alone told a story of just how hard they worked to get their body into shape for this game. They were corded, muscular, littered with tattoos, mouthwater—

NOT the fucking time to be simping over some psycho Ranch rando, Aubrey.

I brought up a hand to slap myself on the face, forcing myself to get my head in the game.

If they're running, I should run too, right?

But the need to kill the Architect fucker was too strong. I turned back to him, ready to push the spike further into his chest, but then a warm, calloused hand grabbed my hand and yanked me down the hallway.

The fucking cowboy. They were even more massive as they moved in front of me. Even through my anger, my eyes narrowed in on their muscular back. I imagined how good it would feel to run my hands down it.

And my fans would go crazy for it. Watching someone as big as them dominate me?

I never had a co-star on the channel before, but they were making me reconsider things.

"Are you an idiot? He has a fucking bounty on him!" I yelled at them and attempted to jerk my hand away, but they were too strong.

Fuck. I love dominant partners.

They didn't look back at me as they yelled, "So what? He's a shit person, there's nothing satisfying in going after him. You'll get more money when you cross the finish line!"

I looked back at where we had left Hiram, ready to yell every curse in the book at him and promise to come back and cut off his head, but paused when I saw what we were *actually* running from. *Water.*

It had started as a trail behind the rats, but then it quickly turned into a strong current.

I was jerked into the same hallway the mechanical bulls had come from as they pulled us far away from the water. I clearly wasn't running fast enough because the cowboy got annoyed with my pace and pulled me into their arms. But it was too late. The stream just got stronger, the water crashing against the walls and following us.

I looked back to see Hiram attempting to follow us.

"What your fucking han—"

I was cut off by a monstrous wave coming straight for us. Hiram's face was the last thing I saw before it rushed in and knocked us Weston and I off our feet.

CAM

CRAB BOIL

Some people just didn't use the good sense that God graced them with.

The blonde's outfit was suggestive, barely coverin' her chest with thick pink straps attached to the scrap of fabric that the stylists had dared allege was a skirt. In a different setting, it would've been the sort of thing that would've earned a low whistle and the offer of a free drink. But down here? I barely had time to think before I was pullin' the girl into my arms to get away from the water threatening to pull us down.

She was too slow, especially when she kept wanting to go back for that Architect.

Bloodthirsty little woman. I might've been running, but I could tell how rabid she was when I first saw her with him. Even behind the mask, her eyes were alight with anger. Her hand was steady when she held the spike over his chest.

She never wavered.

A woman like that would do well in the Games. *And back home.* Pa would arrange the wedding him-fuckin'-self if I ever took someone like her home. He wanted me to be happy, wanted me to succeed, but most importantly, he wanted the family's legacy to continue. Having someone like her at my side would ensure that the future of our family's legacy wouldn't just survive but thrive.

I lost my footin' as the water caught up to us, swept around a bend quickly enough that I cracked my head and elbow against the stone walls and let go of the pretty blonde.

Pain ricocheted throughout my head and black spots sprouted across my vision. It was enough to make me lose my thoughts, even for just a moment before getting my shit back together.

Fuck. An injury like this can take me out for good if I'm not careful.

Ella and I'd been separated at some point, taking opposite directions in our mad dash to find higher ground. Which there didn't seem to be any of. Just miles and miles of flat land that was still rapidly fillin' with water.

Fuckin' hell, you'd think they really are tryin' to drown us.

What a boring way to knock out some of the competition. Not much of a show—there wouldn't even be any blood.

The girl wasn't far from me, but the current kept sweeping her up, and she was strugglin' to swim against it.

Again the voice in my head that sounded strangely like Pa told me to leave her, but I used it as a sign that the opposite was probably the right thing to do.

"Grab hold!" I ordered the blonde, offerin' my hand. She hesitated, a look of mistrust in her light blue eyes before grabbin' on.

It turned out that self-preservation often won out in times like this, and sure, I wasn't perfect, but I could sure as shit swim. Every year Pa forced me and my siblings into the freezing cold lake on the outside of our farm and had us swim laps until our lips were blue and our toes threatened to fall off.

This was a far cry from the terror of those times, so even with my injury and poundin' head, I was sure to be fine.

I wrapped my arms around her slim body and pulled her as close as I could to me. We were swept along, our bodies twisting and jerking as the water took us along.

I tried to open my eyes and see where we were going, but it

became murky, and I honestly thought it was safer to close my eyes than risk an infection.

My back hit the concrete walls more than a few times, and that threatened to pull the air from my lungs. Each time my grip got looser and looser on the woman until it was by the grace of her tiny arms wrappin' around my neck that she was able to stay on.

Water entered my nose, burnin' as it forced its way through my system.

Just as the final bit of air was about to escape my lips, we were spat out into a room, not unlike the one I'd set off the fuckin' water trap to begin with, hittin' the ground with enough force to knock the small bit of air out of my lungs.

The little blonde's body landed on top of mine.

It felt good. Her heat sinking into mine. Her lithe fingers running down my chest. We melded together with the ease.

Maybe it was the adrenaline from almost dyin'... but I dare say her body felt like it *belonged* against mine

Electricity shot through me as my fingers twitched against her back. Her blonde locks tickling my face. Beyond the scent of the water and maze stench, was her sweet, floral perfume.

Lilies. The scent traveled through me and embedded in my brain. It quickly became my favorite scent.

She recovered faster than I did, jumpin' to her feet in the rapidly filling room, backing away quickly, her hands in the air as if trying to protect herself from an incoming blow.

No. Her movements rung my heart out.

"Don't come near me!" she yelled, frightened blue eyes moving around the room as she tried to put some distance between us.

I staggered up, the once-cold water quickly warming where it sloshed around my calves and quickly coming up to hit my knees.

I raised my own hands to show her I meant no harm.

"Hey, now, darlin', don't worry—I'm no PK, alright?"

"Bullshit!" she snapped, her glowing pink mask cracked, only half lit in the relative dark of the room.

An alarm began to blare, adding to the rush of water and forcin' me to yell over it. "Yeah, fair enough. Just saved your life back there to bash your skull in, right?"

The water really was getting hotter. At first it was pleasant, but then it quickly started to make me sweat. Not only that—it was slowly changin' color, and there was a certain metallic smell wafting through the room.

What the fuck?

"Well, how the fuck am I supposed to know? You're a fucking stranger!" she shouted back, stumbling a little as the floor beneath us began to move, slowly rising in segments. Pillars.

There were about seven of them spaced out around the room, some further than others. Before I could think of which one might be the best to take strategically, I realized what the water was turning into.

It was turning a dark red and becoming thicker until it was hard to sift through it.

It's fuckin' blood.

I didn't have time to think about which pillar to take. If I didn't get out of the water that instant, my entire body would be soaked in boilin' blood.

I jumped onto the nearest one, relieved to be lifted from the sweltering warmth. I looked down at her as my pillar was rising. Her eyes were still watchin' me with that same mistrust even after I saved her life.

Valid, though. I wouldn't trust me either. These Games weren't time to make friends. And it was likely whoever got close to you in there was likely to be your downfall.

"Okay, well, my name is Cam. What's yours?"

I took my mask off, hopefully showing her that she could trust me, even just a little bit. I threw it into the blood, the lights blinkin' out as it sank into the thick liquid.

Her eyes were on me for just a second before she was back staring at the blood.

I stood up, shakily trying to wipe off the blood from my skin. It was starting to stick to me.

"Fuck, is this blood? *Disgusting.*"

She scrambled to get up onto a platform before the blood reached her skirt. After she was safely on the pillar, she looked at me again, staying silent until—

"Aubrey," she replied tersely, looking down at the rising liquid. It matched the progress of the pillars, churning at the closed door. Steam began to rise from its surface, warning of the temperature below.

In just a few moments, the blood will be boiling.

The heat of it had beads of sweat running down my face. The air was sticky, hard to breathe. *And that fucking smell...*

"Okay, well, now there, darlin'. Aren't strangers anymore, are we? First name basis and everythin'."

Most importantly, we need to get out of this fuckin' disgusting death trap.

Her eyes narrowed on me, recognition spreading across her features. She dabbed a bit of sweat off her neck before pointing a finger at me.

"Hey, wait a minute, aren't you from the Legacy family that, like, owns cattle or something? Like on a real-life farm? Weston, right?"

Like on a real-life farm. I wanted to laugh at how outrageous the conversation was turning.

My gaze shot around the room as steam threatened to obscure my vision. *Yes, this is exactly what I want to talk about right now.*

"Something like that, darlin'," I said and forced another smile even though she couldn't see it. "But I think we have more impo—"

Aubrey's foot slipped on the slick surface of the pillar just enough for her foot to dip into the liquid, making her yelp as she fell backwards on her platform.

She unsuccessfully tried to fling the blood off her shoe before shooting me a look, anger and shock filling her eyes.

"Crab boil," I answered to her look of furious confusion. "Start 'em cold and then raise the temperature slow so they don't notice until it's too late, otherwise they'll use each other to climb out."

"With fucking blood? Twisted fucked-up Architects," she mumbled under her breath. "So how do we get out?" Her gaze shot to the door. The platforms had come to a grinding halt, still too far away for either of us to easily reach the doors alone, the gap open and waiting for us.

"If you can trust me to come to you, I could lift you up... but you'll need to pull me up after, yeah?"

She appeared to consider it for a few moments, tossing her ruined mask aside into the blood, where it rapidly sank to the bottom, the pink lights blinking out.

Goddamn. The breath was forced from my lungs when I caught sight of her face.

She was just as beautiful as I thought she'd be behind the mask. Blue eyes, full lips, a heart-shaped face. Her personality nowhere near matched her looks.

Aubrey looked like a pretty cheerleader who should have been on the sidelines at a football game, not in a fucked-up murder maze getting her hands dirty.

No wonder she got close enough to the Architect to almost kill him.

But she was just so... *fucking perfect.* The little voice in the back of my head kept telling me she would be a perfect candidate to take back home.

Another told me that bringing her home would be a mistake cause then I'd have to *share* her. That dark part of me didn't want to share her. It wanted her all to myself.

"Alright."

My heart skipped a beat in my chest at her agreement.

"Alright," I whispered back and gave her a nod.

I needed to get my head back in the game, so I had to force myself to stop looking at her.

I backed up as far as I could on the platform before taking it at a run, jumping to reach her pillar with a skid that nearly sent me right over the edge. Her manicured hand on my forearm wouldn't have been enough to hold me back if I were to take a disastrous fall, but the thought of her trying to save me felt nice.

A buzz rang out, and then our pillar jerked forward. The one closest to us jerked to the left, moving further and further away from us.

Shit.

"Now they're just fuckin' with us," I whispered under my breath.

"All for the show," Aubrey agreed, her eyes carefully watching the way the pillars moved.

The exit wasn't far, but tryin' to jump between moving pillars with blood sticking to our clothes and shoes was a terrifying thought.

"Right, left, left, then up," Aubrey said, her eyes not moving from the moving pillars. Buzz after buzz rang out, warnin' us they'd be movin'. But it was all too fast.

I followed her gaze, watchin' the pillars. *It was a sequence.*

"You sure about that?" I asked, not able to make out the sequence she was seeing.

Her head snapped to me.

"Time for you to take a chance on me," she replied, giving me a wink before jumping to the next pillar.

I cursed under my breath because as soon as she landed, it jerked further away from me.

"Jump on my command and we will get out of here, okay?" she said. My pause had her lettin' out an annoyed groan. "Fucking move your ass!"

Her yell reverberated around the room and had my body moving before my mind caught up to what I was doin'.

I ran at the pillar, jumpin' and flyin' through the air to land just in time for it to move back to its original place. I let out a tense breath and looked up at the blonde knockout who was staring down at me with a cruel smirk.

"*Good girl.*"

Her tone sent a zap of excitement through me.

I looked at the next pillar, and then suddenly, the sequence clicked.

"Can you keep up, darlin'?" I shot her a smile before jumping to the next one.

I didn't even have time to steady myself before her body collided with mine. Her hands wrapped around my shoulders and her chest pushed up to my back. A light laughter rang in my ears.

"The question is, can you?"

And with that, she was jumpin' to the next. This time, she didn't wait for me to follow.

I looked back down at the blood coming up fast and bubbling. The smell was overwhelming and threatened to gag me.

With a deep breath, I jumped the last two pillars before pulling her to me.

"Ready?" I asked, looking down at her.

She let out a playful scoff before pushing me away to turn around to look up at the exit.

"I'll lift ya," I offered a bit too eagerly.

"Keep your hands where they're meant to be, cowboy." Aubrey said with a grin as my hands grabbed her waist. Her fingers grazed the ledge, her heeled boot making hard contact with my chest as she pulled herself up, rolling onto the ledge.

Bitter disappointment coated my tongue. *Am I the only one feeling this?*

The buzzer rang again, warning that the pillars would be shifting.

"Now me," I called up to her, my hands outstretched for a much-needed boost.

She looked over the edge of the door, a feral smile covering her beautiful features. "What was it that Scar said to Mufasa? 'Long live the king'?"

My heart raced, jaw falling slack at her betrayal.

If my life wasn't on the line, I might have taken a moment to revel in just how breathtaking her cruelty was.

There I was, trapped in a pit with only a crab's death awaitin' me, stupid enough to trust a little mouse of a girl to hold up her end of the bargain.

She was meant for the Games more than I was. A fact my subconscious had figured out first when it was daydreaming of bringing her home to Ma and Pa.

If only my survival instincts rang the alarm bells first.

The platform began to lower, blood rushin' onto its surface, threatenin' to swallow me whole. Inch by inch, gettin' me closer to a very painful, very hot death.

Is this how it ends? My family watchin' as the very last of their line is cooked alive because they trusted the wrong person?

Embarrassment and shame filled me faster than my fear of death.

Then, a manicured hand appeared over the edge, and I watched Aubrey lying flat on her stomach, reaching down for me.

Maybe my subconscious was actually right for the first time.

Hope ran through my body, and a smile spread across my face.

I let out a laugh then jumped up, catching her wrists and using my feet against the wall to help pull myself up. With a considerable amount of effort from both of us, and with only a little bit of melted rubber on the soles of my boots, we lay side by side on the solid stone floor of the next corridor, panting hard.

But we weren't fully out of the woods yet. There was a wall separatin' us from the rest of the maze.

Tears slid down Aubrey's cheeks in fat droplets, smearing her makeup and making her nose red.

Poor girl. Maybe she isn't as bloodthirsty as I first thought.

The Games did things to people, including turnin' them into monsters. Maybe she too had a soft spot inside her.

"Hey now, darlin', it's okay. We made it."

"No, you don't get it. There was a girl back there—"

"Shh, c'mon, we can't save 'em all. They know what they're gettin' into signing up for a thing like this, right?"

"I don't care that she's dead, Cam, I care that I didn't get to kill her! That stupid fucking cunt was the whole reason I signed up for this shitshow, and now I have NOTHING! No reason to be here! No reason to want to win! She won't even get to see me holding the trophy!"

Christ on a cracker, this girl is nuttier than a buckeye.

And after that performance... I owed her my life.

Fucking hell.

AUBREY
FUCK, COULD I BE ANY HORNIER?

They looked at me like I was crazy.

Well, to be exact, all expression dropped from their face, and I was met with a deadpan stare, but given their previous demeanor, I was guessing this was some type of mental break for them.

Fuck, they are hot.

I knew they were as soon as I saw the toned, tattooed arms, but holy fuck, their face card was lethal. Plump lips, chiseled jaw, straight nose. All the features just came together to create a perfect semi-masculine face that had me wanting to drop to my knees in front of them.

They could stomp on me with their booted foot, call me every dirty name under the sun, spit on me—fuck, the thought actually has my pussy clenching—and I would beg for more.

"You have literally no other goal?" they asked with a cocked brow.

I shook my head, tears still streaming down my face. I couldn't stop them. After all the work I put into it, after everything I did to get to her, after everything she had done to me.

Maybe it was almost dying in a pit of boiling blood that finally brought the emotions out of me.

"No!" I cried, desperately trying to wipe them off my face without ruining my makeup more than it already was. Another thing I had worked so hard on that she was ruining even after she was fucking dead. "You don't get it! She was a huge fucking cunt and this was my only way to get back at her and now she's dead and I wasn't even the one to do it!"

Another silence followed by water dripping somewhere in the room.

"Well, I have a goal," they said and rolled their shoulders, their eyes looking over the well-placed trap. I let my eyes trail down their body. The tank top was pulled tight against their skin and made my mouth water. It made me feel just a bit better about Natalie's death. Fuck, could I be any hornier? "And I need you to obtain it, so can you please stop with this tantrum and come help me?"

Tantrum?

My inner simping came to a screeching halt. I sniffled, trying to stop the tears.

Being scolded by Cam ignited something in me that made me want to obey but also do the exact opposite and see what they would do. I wanted to see a bit more of the frustration and anger I saw peeking through in their eyes. I wanted to provoke them.

I wanted them to use those strong arms of theirs and pin me up against the wall and—

"Tell me what your goal is, then," I said with a sniffle, pushing the dirty thoughts to the back of my head. They gave me another deadpan look. "Please?"

"*No.*" They walked further into the corridor, bending down so they were closer to the ground. There was a wall separating us and the rest of the maze. Their hand slid across the ground, checking for an opening. "Trust me, if I didn't need your help, I wouldn't be askin'."

"Then tell me," I replied with a whine and pushed myself up from the floor.

When they didn't turn to me, I leaned over their back, putting my weight on them and using them as some sort of stool. Under the stink of blood, they had a distinct woodsy smell that had my stomach clenching.

It was undeniable.

I want them.

Natalie was slowly disappearing into the recesses of my mind while Cam was worming their way in. It was useless to try and stop it. I could feel it coming on stronger than anything I had ever felt for Natalie.

"So you can stab me in the back just before I reach it?" they asked.

I let out a groan and buried my face into their neck. Their hair tickled my face. I had the urge to sink my teeth into the muscled column.

"Come on," I cooed. "Tell me and I'll help you."

They let out a heavy sigh.

"It's the family business," they said in a low voice. "I am the last of all my siblings to enter the Games. I don't have a choice. I have to win."

I mulled over their words. They were... more interesting than that bastard Hiram for sure. And their goal was just so... *cute.*

I mean, every time the Games came around, there were those who entered as Legacies. Their families counting on them to continue the line of succession and win, no matter the cost.

But the way they said it...

It felt like Cam didn't truly want to win. Like they were doing it just to shut their family up.

But that doesn't mean they're not good at it.

And I had heard the rumors of how their family worked. They were well known. They trained hard. Produced perfectly bred children that were *born* to win the Games.

It wasn't often that they *weren't* part of the winners' pool.

Yet Cam seemed... different. And I wanted to know why.

"Okay."

Their head whipped over to look at me, all but pushing me off them in the process. "Really?" they asked.

"Really," I said and placed my palm on the scanner. "Let's just say you moved me."

Cam hesitantly put their hand on the other sensor, and the wall melted away right in front of our eyes.

"Thank you," they whispered as we both stood upright. My heart began pounding in my chest. They looked at me like I was some type of savior. The power of that made my head spin.

I leaned in close, smiling up at them.

"I think I deserve something," I teased. "After all, I'm the only one who can help you achieve those big dreams of yours."

The way redness spread across their face and neck caused something to flip inside my stomach.

All the madness of what happened earlier in the maze was gone. Hiram and the girl he killed were but a passing spec of dust. Unimportant if not a bit annoying. Even if only for a moment.

All I wanted was to see what other reactions I could pull from them. See what was hidden behind that front of theirs.

The thought almost made me pause. *Natalie.* Her name was Natalie. The girl who fucked over my entire life yet somehow she had been replaced by the Weston.

I can't even bring myself to care.

"Cam?" a voice called from the open doorway.

I didn't look to see who it was, but I did catch the pure joy on their face as they took in the newcomer.

Joy that should have been reserved for the person who was helping them win.

I gritted my teeth, my gaze following Cam as they pushed past me to greet the newcomer.

I paused, taking her in. She wasn't just any random runner.

It's the bitch in the dressing room!

"Aubrey, this is Ella; Ella, Aubrey. We met when we were running—"

"How are you even alive?" Ella asked, bewildered. Even

though she was rude enough to cut Cam off, they didn't seem to mind. Cam let out a laugh and slapped their hand on her shoulder.

The personal nature of their interaction had me gritting my teeth.

I literally just saved your life and you're chatting up other girls already? And that bitch in particular?

"You didn't think you could get rid of me that easily, did you?" they asked and continued walking down the new hallway.

Ella looked at me, surprise flashing across her face, before something like hesitancy followed it. *That's right. Think twice about your place here.*

But there was something else odd about her. The look on Ella's face told me that she *had* thought they could get rid of them that easily.

Hm.

I followed behind Cam, sending a glare at Ella. *I would be the one helping Cam with their dream.* And *they* didn't feel right to me.

A ping from my tracker had me looking down.

Vic_Official: *Don't Trust. Danger.*

Vic. Why risk sending me this message?

I quickly hid it and watched as the two walked ahead of me. I trusted Vic enough to tell me the truth about my party, but the issue was...

Who exactly was the danger?

Cam

We don't PK, remember?

It was something not unlike relief to see Ella again. It wasn't that I felt any kind of way about the girl—despite being pretty, she wasn't really my type. Nah, that was all Aubrey.

Blonde, golden tan, big, beautiful blue eyes that went on forever. That was more my speed. Even if she seemed a bit off her rocker.

And there was just a sort of... connection between us.

I didn't need to pull her along with me. Or help her in the blood room. Or really do anything other than try to win.

But I wanted to.

Not only did I want to, but it came second nature to me.

Even as we were walking through the maze, my attention kept turning to the blonde.

But Ella was something like a friend, even if she had ditched me to go the other direction earlier. It was easy to get caught up in the maze, to make calls or split-second decisions that didn't quite meet the expectations we had for ourselves. Besides, I sort of felt responsible for her since we accidentally became a duo after I saved her life from that first-floor trap.

My watch buzzed, but I ignored it, reaching back to catch

Aubrey's hand and forcing her clenched fist apart to hold her little palm in mind.

But even through the connection, I was... uncertain about her. She was smart, there was no doubt. But she was also a loose cannon, someone who would be difficult to control. And situations I couldn't control? Those were dangerous. They needed immediate and brutal resolution.

It was the only way. And Aubrey didn't seem like the person who would appreciate a brutal resolution.

My gaze shot to her, rememberin' the wicked smile she gave me as she held my life in her lithe hands back in the blood room.

Or maybe that's exactly the type of thing she likes. And just maybe, I wanted to find out more of what made the beautiful bombshell tick.

"C'mon," I said, taking a few steps until her unmoving body made her arm go taut. "Let's go this way, there is still a lot of ground to cover."

It was concerning that we hadn't run into many other players yet. Made me worry that we were going the wrong way, or worse, that we were already so far behind that someone was already closin' in on the finish line.

Anxiety flicked in my chest, my fingers tightenin' around Aubrey's.

If I lost this, I was a fucking goner. Especially if I lost this because I'd tied myself to a couple of spoiled brats that didn't even want to win.

Fuck.

C'mon, Cam, head in the game.

Aubrey's narrowed eyes slid from Ella back to me, forcing a tight smile as she stepped closer, her free hand fluffing her Aurora-like hair. Seriously, who looked like *that*? She giving Disney princess vibes even after getting positively drenched in blood was... a feat to say the least. For a moment, I almost forgot Ella was there.

"No, I think we should go east."

"East?" I echoed. "I'm pretty sure that we are veering too far from the middle as is... If we try to continue east, we might end up hittin' the border wall and getting stuck. Or worse, have to waste time backtrackin'."

"But—"

"God," Aubrey snapped, tugging my hand as she moved to go west. "If you have a problem with it, just go off on your own then. We don't need you anyway."

Her harshness caused my heart to skip a beat.

Fuck, I shouldn't like that as much as I do.

"Aubrey," I chastised, even as I followed her. "We should stick together if we can."

Privately, as much as I hated it, I knew that larger groups got more views, which meant more hints and an easier path to the goal. Like they were trying to prove my point, my watch buzzed again, drawing my attention.

Vic_Official: *WEST!*

Vic. The name stuck out to me. Only after. Moment did I realize that Vic meant Victoria and I had suddenly been graced with a message from one of Hide N' Seek's most watched contestant. Her and that blonde person had taken the stream by storm. Admittedly I also tuned in to watch a bit of their game but quickly had to turn it off when the blonde's moans filtered through the speakers.

I held up my watch so that Ella could see the message. Aubrey saw it, her face lighting up.

"That's my girl," she said with a wicked grin. "Sorry, rat, over-ruled. Now, c'mon, we need to make up some time."

Aubrey kicked off into an impatient jog, and I followed, passing by turns with little thought. I wasn't sure how much of it was a power move, an educated guess, or just pure instinct that was moving her. Ella struggled, irritated, to follow us.

We took turns, finding dead ends several times before the thin hallway we'd been following opened into a large antechamber with a fountain and plants.

The room was large, probably about the size of a department store, with lush, deeply overgrown flower beds filled with blooms in many colors and giant fern bushes and trees. An explosion of color that made it hard to look at them too long.

I blinked hard at the sudden saturation in the room, overwhelmed as much by the smell, so different from the dampish, earthen musk of the maze, as by the sudden all-consuming bath of apparent sunlight overhead. It couldn't be. We were miles under the ground and ocean, but I couldn't look up long enough to get a good look anyway. There were screens all around, each of them scrolling through all the runners in the maze and their current rankings.

A large circular fountain sat in the middle of the room, gazebos dotted around with places to sit and vending machines. Above us, facing the opposite wall, were four metal gates.

A large, red button stood on a pedestal in front of them.

Randomization? They'd never done that before—chosen which path you would take to the finale.

It didn't sit right.

I paused to look at mine, but Aubrey let out an excited noise that had my attention moving to her. She was running to a large metal box that had a bunch of light-up buttons on it.

"It's a vending machine!" she said excitedly. "There's even a machete in here!"

"We're at the center," I stated, looking around at the room. The fountain was large. So large I couldn't see behind it. But I could *hear* something.

Voices.

My hackles raised. Slowly, leaving Aubrey behind, I sneaked around the fountain.

The screens lit up the room, but without giving enough light for me to make out a figure. I hadn't noticed that we weren't alone. Or the color of the water. But as soon as I rounded the corner, I saw it right away.

There was a body nailed to the other side of the fountain by its hands and arms. Nailed might be the wrong word. Four large metal stakes were driven into the body and one large machete went right through the chest, pinning it to the fountain.

The most eye-catching thing, though, was the head—or lack thereof.

It had been sliced right off. It was so fresh, blood still fell down from the wound on the neck and into the water, dying it red.

On the lip of the fountain sat the head, the expression on the player's face censored by a bright green mask, but their eyes were wide and terrified.

There was a group of five standing to the side and talking excitedly. They quieted a bit when they saw me.

My blood ran cold when I saw what was painted on the ground in the player's blood.

Make a show of it.

The darkness in my mind had pushed itself to the forefront, reminding me of my duty. It was like the offering had been placed right in front of me as a warnin'.

You can never leave us. God is watching.

Not only was God watching, but his followers were reminding me of just how far I had fallen from his grace.

I should have been the one to make this offering. *I* should have been the one to introduce Pa's practice to the world.

It was the perfect forum. *But he got there first.*

My eyes fell to the group. *Elijah.* Not only had he beat me to the maze, but he had made an offering as well.

When I saw him in the lineup, I knew he would get far... *but before me?*

The darkness told me to turn *him* into an offering. To prove to both Pa and God that I was the true chosen that would bring honor to our practice.

We don't PK. The words swirled around in my head. They reminded me that I didn't want to be like them. That I had come in here just to win and have that be enough.

But He was testing me.

Elijah's mask was off and placed on the side of his head, revealing his freckled nose and slightly crooked teeth. He gave me a sinister smile.

What I hadn't expected was Hiram to be hiding behind Elijah. He was keeping him around for a payout at the end. No doubt Hiram would end up as an offering.

Fuckin' genius. Wish I'd thought of it.

The darkness slunk to the back when Aubrey came up to me. She had been saying something but stopped when she reached me.

Aubrey stiffened at the sight of the offering.

In that moment, I missed my mask. It would've been nice to have even a little anonymity when it came to meeting other players. The hazard of having a famous family was that there were more than enough people who were pissed at us for either accidentally or on purpose killing their loved ones. Or sometimes they just wanted to knock us down a peg. Somethin' about being famous forever for killin' one of us. That's what happened with Billy, Lord keep him.

Snuffed out for some dipshit's ego. The headlines made me fuckin' sick.

Though my tattoos and overall build would have given me away to most people who knew of me. The mask was a privilege *other* people had.

"What the actual fresh hell is that? Someone decided to decorate this fugly-ass place?"

Praying for Aubrey to keep her mouth shut would have been a waste, so instead I prayed that the angel sent to test me would find mercy on me. Which, all things considered, was probably a bit of a waste of time too.

"Well, well, well," Elijah called, a dark eyebrow climbing toward his hairline. "I wondered if we'd get to run into you, Cam."

"Elijah," I said, acknowledged him as I offered my most

award-winnin' smile, pulling Aubrey into my side, my arm going possessively around her shoulders. I hoped she'd get the memo that we needed to tread lightly.

Elijah isn't one to fuck with. No one from the farm was. Though I hope he saw her as an opportunity instead of the dangerous temptation she really was.

But that was hope that died instantly the minute the blonde opened her sinful mouth again.

"Way to sound like a two-bit backwoods super villain wannabe. Any other exciting anecdotes you'd like to provide?"

Damn it.

Her tongue was sharp. In any other situation, I would have loved to hear it, but this wasn't the place. Not when we were face-to-face with a group that outnumbered us and a fresh offering to our left.

"You really should train your bitch not to talk back, Cam," quipped another player, tossing her short hair back.

Bad move. I realized that when Aubrey shook my arm away and went right up to the player who insulted her. I could feel the anger rolling off her in waves. One more wrong move, and I might get a glimpse of just how bloodthirsty she could be.

"Yeah, like I give a fuck what a cunt with a fuck ass bob has to say, but thanks. If you'll excuse us, we have a game to win."

The group bristled. Ella, who had been slowly moving around the fountain, shifted closer to my side at the obvious change of demeanor.

Two of the players on either side brandishing large metal baseball bats started moving toward us.

Elijah was there, watchin' it all go down. There was a superior feel to his aura. Like I was nothing but a cockroach under his shoe instead of the daughter of the family who took him in and trained him for that very moment. He should've been thankful I showed up.

If anything, he owes me!

"Now, now," Elijah, the *de facto* group leader, said, standing up with a languid stretch of his arms over his head. "No need for all of that, right? We're the first group to pass through the center zone. Look above you."

Kill him. Prove that you're better than him. That he can't talk to you that way. Then take the Architect for yourself.

Killing Hiram as an offering could fix every single one of my problems. Winning would pale in comparison.

No PK. No PK. No PK. Focus on somethin' else. Anythin'.

I had to chant it in my head to stop myself from acting on the impulse to kill him. My eyes didn't move for the weapons that were serving now as more than a warning; they were an obvious threat.

"Oh my God," Ella whispered beside me excitedly. "I'm in eighth."

I did the mental math. That meant I was either in sixth or seventh, depending on how things had shaken out between Aubrey and me for who got more points.

Fuck.

Still podium-worthy, but now I was relatively unarmed and faced with five hostiles with only two untrained civilians as support.

I'm a fuckin' embarrassment.

It felt like I was being punished. Hiram could fix that.

"Shut up," I whispered to myself. No one looked twice at me, thankfully not hearing me.

I clenched my fists and gritted my teeth. *I will make it work.* It wasn't the worst odds I could've had, but fuck me, they weren't brilliant either.

"As if," Aubrey huffed. "Step aside so we can pass, losers."

"The only loser I see here is you," Fuck Ass Bob said, sneering. "So pathetic walking around like a fucking billboard. What, was Times Square already booked?"

Aubrey, to my surprise, laughed, rolling her sapphire eyes. "Oooooooooh, I'm soooo bad. I see another woman getting a bag and I can't help but be jealous. God, you're so pathetic. Bet you wouldn't have half the balls to pipe up to me if you weren't kicking it with half the cast of the Power Rangers."

She was up faster than I'd pegged her for, crossing the short distance on the gravel to get up in Aubrey's face, her own round cheeks flamin'. "Say that again, Polly Pocket."

Elijah shifted, his eyes on the two at my side. I wanted to watch Aubrey. Maybe even help. But he was more dangerous than anyone else in the room.

"Feeling awful safe, aren't you?" Aubrey said, her lip curling in disgust at the closeness. "Can you please back up? You seriously need a mint."

Was love for continual insults a thing?

Like a fucked-up love at first sight but instead born out of watchin' someone repetitively dress somebody down. I shouldn't have been so turned on by it, but her darkness was speaking to mine.

It reached out slowly, showin' itself in the littlest of ways.

In her speech.

In the way she whined about not killin' her long-time nemesis.

In the way she had looked like she was going to kill Hiram when she had the chance.

There was so much more to her.

Fuck me, Aubrey is... somethin' else.

"You want to talk about being brave?" the girl said, spitting at Aubrey's feet. "Attaching yourself to a Legacy with more tattoos than they have brain cells—oh, sorry, Cam, brain cells are the gooey pink stuff that makes it so that you can have enough aware- ness to Hulk-smash your fist into things in the hopes that—"

Smack.

Well, actually, it was more like *crunch* as Aubrey's fist connected with the girl's face, positively shattering her nose in an explosion of blood that splattered all three of us as well as the ground.

My mouth popped open in surprise, but I barely had time to

think about reactin' before the two with large bats were moving toward us.

I grabbed ahold of the lasso hanging off my pants and ran at them. It worked. They startled, not expectin' me to jump into action as fast as I did.

I threw the rope at their feet as they stumbled back and pulled, tyin' them together like I was ropin' calves. It was enough to force both of them off their feet and to the ground. One of them dropped their bat, but the other was quick to push himself up.

He tried to come at me, but with the other player still attached to him at the ankle, his bat missed my body by a whole foot. I used my chance to grab it and clock him right in the head with it, knockin' him out.

"Hey, Cam," the other said fearfully, raising his hand. "I didn't mean anything—"

I slammed my body into his, throwing us to the ground.

Elijah was still staring at the scene, unmoving. I met his gaze hard and ready to fight, but a sound called me back to Aubrey.

She's going to fuckin' kill her.

"Aubrey, get off her!" I shouted, on top of the larger of the two and forcing his face into the gravel, readyin' the bat. "We aren't PKers, remember?"

"YOU aren't a PKer," Aubrey corrected, satisfaction washing over her face as the girl grew increasingly purple the longer her hands were wrapped around her throat.

Aubrey was scratched up everywhere—arms and hands, neck and face—anywhere the girl could reach in her increasingly feebler attempts to get her off her. She bucked her hips but didn't do much more than make my girl adjust.

Ella screamed as Elijah took his chance and chased her around the fountain. He paused when he saw Aubrey, shifting his focus.

Hiram is out in the open. It was a chance that wouldn't come around again. *Priorities. Focus on your people.*

A loud crack and a splash.

Fuck. Okay. Priorities shiftin'.

Using the bat, I struck the struggling body underneath me in the temple until he stopped moving, jumping at the body that was trying to pull Aubrey off the girl, the bat clatterin' down near her knee.

She was screaming so loud it was hard to think, her frustrated noises drawing my attention to how she might sound wrapped around my fingers.

No time, Cam. Focus.

I was so scatterbrained that I hadn't realized the first player I knocked out was already at my back, wrappin' his arm around my neck and attemptin' to put a knife to my throat.

I rolled in the gravel, trying to get the upper hand on my new opponent. Luckily for me, they were drastically outmatched in size, but unluckily for me, I was being too cocky when a knife slashed into my cheek, close enough to my eye to make it water.

Splashes and the sound of struggle followed me as my ears began to ring, grabbin' the player's arm and forcin' it under my knee. Giving it as little thought as I could, I braced their hand and elbow, snapping it like a glow stick. He screamed, and I jumped to my feet, adequately convinced he was incapacitated enough for me to try to check on Ella.

Shaking my head to dislodge a bit of the blood that was slicking down my face, I looked at Aubrey, and she was holding her own, so I jogged around the side of the fountain to find Elijah sitting on top of Ella.

My watch buzzed, the lights in the room flickering down into near darkness for a few terrifying seconds as I jumped into the basin of the fountain, the screens flashing red Xs warning that a PK had just happened.

Fuck. Fuck!

I jumped on Elijah's back, rippin' him off the body that was no longer struggling under the water.

I pushed away the worry that my family would disown me for my actions. *No PK. Help them.*

"Ella!" I shouted, turning and struggling to lift her head out of the water as I was being dragged backwards by Elijah, his furious grip trying to stop me from getting to her.

Her dark hair appeared over the water, splutterin' and coughin'.

Relief. I couldn't have a teammate die on my watch.

Then who…?

"Aubrey!" I shouted, fully engagin' with Elijah now, grapplin' with him as he tried to force my head underwater.

I had gone up against many from the farm, but never under the duress that my own personal angel was about to die.

Another flash of the lights and another shower of red Xs above us, the leaderboard changing rapidly, numbers fallin' away as fallen players were accounted for. Names moving by so quickly that I couldn't figure out who was gone.

"AUBREY!"

"Oh my God, keep your fucking cowboy hat on, Cam," she snapped, the screaming from the player whose arm I'd broken suddenly cut off, accompanied by another red flash.

Oh my God. She wasn't dying.

She's killin' them.

"Aubrey! Stop!" I ordered as Elijah released me, clearly coming to the same conclusion.

Ella had hauled herself out of the fountain, pounding on her chest to try and dislodge the bloodied water from her lungs as she coughed it up.

I hopped over the stone lip, grateful again for my size as I overtook it easily, grabbin' Aubrey around the middle and hauling her bodily off the tied-up player whose head she was about to bash in with the metal bat. I ran full tilt with her under my arm like she weighed less than a football, stopping only to pull Ella onto my back before crossing the room to the button, my hand jammin' down onto it desperately.

Three. She'd PKed three people in a no-PK zone.

And we'd left two of their friends alive. One of them fuckin' trained for the Games.

Fuck. Fuck. Fuck.

This is not how I wanted my game to go. *Tests come to those who are worthy.* But I didn't feel worthy. Especially not when Aubrey was threatenin' to fuck it all up.

The middle-left door opened, and I was quick to get through it, turnin' my head to adjust a slipping Ella and catching sight of the two remaining players. But it shut too quickly. I froze, waitin' to see if pressing the button would open the door again... but nothing. Seconds ticked by—ten, twenty, thirty—before I let loose a relaxed breath.

"Are you going to put me down now?" Aubrey snapped.

I saw red. This mouthy little brat needed to be taught a lesson about listenin'. And I was gonna be the one to do it.

Aubrey

Manners, darlin'.

I *did my best to save us, so why the fuck is Cam so mad at me?* They've been all but ignoring me since we ran into the bloodthirsty player group.

It wasn't my fault. They were asking to die.

And, if anything, Cam should have been happy about it, given how much of the competition I killed for them. Who would have thought that Kohl's dad would have somehow found a place for himself next to the only other person from the Ranch in the maze.

I should have killed Hiram when I had the chance. That weasel somehow got accepted into a group and was probably going to be a huge pain in the fucking ass.

"Let's stop for a break," Ella said, looking back at both Cam and me. She was breathing heavily, still winded by Cam pulling her through the maze at breakneck speed.

I didn't try to hide my distaste for her. *She's just fucking annoying.* And I heard Cam scream her name *first* before they decided to check on me. Which pisses me off even more.

"Break? We need to get to the finish line be—"

"A break sounds nice, actually," Cam said and sank down

onto the floor with their back against the concrete wall. They didn't meet my gaze.

I opened my mouth to protest when a beep sounded. I froze, then quickly relaxed when I saw a service robot coming down the hallway. It held a pack and was coming straight for me.

When it was about a foot away, it stopped and let out a *beep-boop* noise.

With a smile, I reached forward and grabbed the bag. There was a note attached to it. I opened it.

To the lovely Aubrey from your sponsors at LadyPink,

For you and your friends! Inside is our newest, fat-reducing energy bars and electrolyte water for you to enjoy!

With a big smile, I looked out into the empty space of the hallway as the robot retracted, knowing the cameras would catch every moment.

"Thank you, LadyPink, for these delicious treats!"

I made a show of putting the bag on the ground, digging through it, then ripping into one of the snack bars and taking a huge bite.

It was mediocre at best.

I was interrupted by the rat reaching forward and digging into the bag herself. She looked at me with a smile before pulling out a small water bottle and a protein bar. I wanted to pull on that ponytail and bash her face in. My hand clutched the bloodied metal bat I'd stolen from the group.

I frowned when she took a sip and Cam looked at her expectantly. She looked at me and back at them.

"Do you want some?" Ella asked, tilting the bottle to Cam.

"Thanks for offering," they said and reached forward to grab it.

Seriously? Without hesitation?

They were going to put their mouth on something that rat did? *They are practically kissing at this point!*

Anger and something else rose in me so fast I couldn't stop my hand from reaching out and slapping the water bottle out of their hands before it could touch their lips.

Cam was silent for what felt like an eternity. The water bottle fell to the ground, rolling away and spilling out some of the liquid.

Ella was just as shocked, but quickly, anger started seeping into her expression.

"Are you fucking kidding me?" Ella asked and reached for it again. "We have no idea how long we're going to be in here, and you want to waste our water? For what? A one-sided grudge?"

"I don't have grudges," I spat. "I don't fucking trust a rat like you. You're a fucking cunt. I'm not even sure why Cam—"

"Okay, that's enough of that," Cam said, their hand finding my arm. "It's *water*. We need it. I'm sure if you had asked, she would have shared with you too."

This time it was my turn for shocked silence.

What the—did they just—

Even my thoughts skidded to a halt.

I had no words. I opened my mouth to speak, but nothing came out. Cam was just staring at me with that innocent-looking face of theirs.

"We need to talk," I finally managed to say and grabbed their arm, forcing them up.

They hesitantly followed me as I took them back down the hallway and around the corner to where the rat couldn't see us.

"Don't let the water—"

"I don't give a shit about the water," I said and spun around so we were both facing each other. "We don't need them. She's slowing us down. Remember why you're here? You have a goal. She wants us to stop so you won't reach your goal."

They looked back over their shoulder—toward the rat—before looking back at me.

"So this is about her stopping me from reaching my goal?" they asked.

I nodded.

"I said I'd help you. Let me help you."

Another long look. I couldn't decipher their expression at all. "Why do you care?"

Why do I care?

Do I... actually care?

It was a loaded question. If I was being honest, I hadn't cared about much in my life other than if my mascara was running or if the viewers on my after-dark channel would continue to pay me.

But caring about this random Ranch Legacy?

A small voice whispered to me that I did. Shockingly, I *did* care.

"I just want you to reach your goal," I said in a softer voice and closed the space between us. We were so close I could feel the heat from their skin. Their breath on my face.

"Then what about back there, huh?" Cam asked, their lips set into a thin line. "Is killing all those people *helping* me?"

Fury rose up in me, coming back with a renewed bite.

"*Yes*," I hissed. "Not only were they insulting you, but killing those people means less competition for *you. I* don't give two shits about winning this stupid ass game."

"Really?" Cam asked, rage threading through their voice. "I don't think you're trying to help me at all. I think you were sent here as a test to distract me from my mission."

This time it was them who took a step forward. I didn't mean to back down, but they were so overwhelming it was an automatic reaction to them towering over me. My legs felt unsteady as I backed away.

A test? I had heard long ago about the special *religion* that the

Ranch used as a control tactic, and with Cam being in the family, there was no doubt they had grown up in that super cult-like belief system.

Had that been how they saw me the whole time?

Even through all the anger, a smile threatened to pull at my lips. Amusement and pride pricked my skin, causing an electrifying current to shoot up my spine.

I'm enough to distract them.

It meant they were watching me, but not just watching. I was *consuming* their thoughts to the point where I was hindering their performance.

"I am trying to help," I huffed. "Getting all philosophical now? If you can't see how I've been breaking my back to help you, that's on you. Everything I did back there was for *you*. You should be grateful."

"You're gonna use that as a way to blame *me* for their deaths?" they asked, their tone turning dangerous. A vicious glint passed their eyes. Their entire body was on edge.

It had my heart racing, my palms sweating.

"I wouldn't have done it if it wasn't for you," I admitted with just as harsh a tone.

The fire that lit their eyes was beautiful. The way their jaw twitched set my body alight. And fuck, all I wanted was for them to show me more of that fiery anger raging behind their warm brown eyes. It was all I could think about. It was so overpowering that it tickled my taste buds.

And everyone is watching.

The after-dark channel I ran was a good way to bring in some good income, but the main reason why I started it in the first place was because I *loved* being watched.

I got high off it. Every time I'd show up in my skimpy clothes and mask to put on a show for my thousands of fans, my heart raced. Feeling their eyes crawling all over me was better than any drug on the market.

They came for my body but stayed for my performance.

Just like with the Games, where people came and put on a show of their lives, I did the same on that channel.

And now they're watching as I simp over a tall muscle mommy who refuses to kill anyone.

"I didn't want to kill anyone," they spat, taking another step forward until I was pushed against the wall. I was cornered. Nowhere to run. And even if I could, they would most likely catch me.

The thought of them chasing me down the maze hallways in nothing but underwear and the promise of what they would do to me when they caught me was quickly becoming my newest fantasy.

"Well, too bad," I hissed and used all my strength to push at their chest.

They didn't even budge. *Fuck, my pussy's throbbing.*

I wanted them to use that strength on me.

"Don't you know what game you're in?" I asked. "People don't come here to act nice, Cam. I thought you'd know that, coming from a Legacy family and all. What will Mommy and Daddy think when they see this replay, huh? Do you think they'll be proud of what a coward their daughter was—"

I was cut off by Cam's large forearm pushing against my neck. The rudeness of it felt like ice cold water had been poured on me. I gasped for air. Tried to kick them. But all they did was lean closer.

I could try all I want, but there was nothing I could do. I was fully and completely under their control.

Fear.

They had actually succeeded in doing something so unexpected that it *scared* me.

And completely turned me on.

"You think just because I won't kill anyone that I can't?"

Their breath was warm across my face. Their lips centimeters from my lips. I darted my tongue out, unable to hold myself back from the need to taste them, and was able to brush across their soft lips before she moved back ever so slightly.

Fuck. My stomach twisted as they applied more pressure to my neck. *Am I really getting turned on by them choking me out in the middle of the maze?*

There was no doubt I was. Even more so, the weight of millions of people watching had me wanting more. It was like the channel on crack.

I might have fantasized about this before, but it could never compare to actually feeling it. My head was spinning, my breath was catching, sweat was dripping from the back of my neck.

The coolness of the stone walls of the maze did nothing to calm my heated skin. Or to make me think twice about what I was going to do.

"You lack the balls," I forced out.

Their eyes narrowed at me. *This was the real Cam.* The one who had been trained their whole life to kill in the Games. The one who wouldn't hesitate to end anyone who got in their way.

"You'd think a pretty thing like yourself would have some fuckin' manners. I saved your life."

"And for what?" I asked. Lifting my face as much as I could. But just as our lips were about to brush, they pulled away. "You seem to just be collecting us *pretty little things.*"

"You're jealous," they accused with a breathy chuckle that went straight to my cunt. Wetness had already been pooling in my underwear since the moment they pushed me against the hard maze wall, and with each second, my body's reaction was becoming more and more indecent.

I pushed against their arm.

"Fuck you. I don't get jealous—"

"Manners, darlin'," they warned, their face leaning close enough that their lips were at my ear. "Or I may just have to teach you a lesson about talkin' back to me."

Their free hand was at my waist, the heat of their fingers seeping through to my skin. I couldn't conceal the shudder.

People are watching, put on a show.

Normally, I would have been able to. I was a fucking star in front of the camera. But Cam's overwhelming presence had rendered me unable to pay attention to anything but them.

They pulled away, gauging my reaction. Their hand moved further down to the edge of my skirt. I didn't know it was possible for my heart to beat faster. Didn't know it was possible for my body to yearn so badly for someone I didn't know.

I want them to fuck me. More than that, I wanted them to destroy me and have all the viewers watch it. I wanted it recorded so that later, when we were out of the maze, they could play back the scene and fuck me even harder to it.

"Is that why you're acting out like this?" they purred. "Are you needy for my attention? Needing me to please you?"

My face heated. Cam sure knew how to push my fucking buttons. But I had a reputation. As turned on as I was, I couldn't just bend to their every command. I might have felt like a bitch in heat, but I didn't need to act like one.

"As if you could," I seethed. "You're clumsy and probably don't even know how to—"

"Now, darlin', we both know that ain't true."

They reached between my legs, their arm still pushing on my throat. My head was getting lighter and lighter, but that only intensified the feeling of their hand coming into contact with my clothed cunt.

They let out a groan that had electricity zapping up my spine.

"You're downright sinful, you know that? A temptation I should never give into."

"Yet here you fucking are," I said, my breathing getting heavier. "You think your god will forgive you for giving in? Or maybe you're too *scared*."

Their eyes flashed. Oh fuck. I should use the god thing more often.

"My own fucking ruin," they whispered, and the words that

were supposed to cut into me like knives felt more like hot, open-mouthed kisses. "Maybe going to hell will be worth it."

Their fingers ran down my folds. There was no teasing anymore. They were touching me. Taking what they wanted. I spread my legs for them, but they just stood there. Staring.

"Are you just going to stand there or are you—"

"Safe word is bubble gum," they hissed. "Now say it so I know you can still breathe."

I gritted my teeth, not wanting to take any direction from them. Pings were going off on my tracker. I could just hear them over the racing of my heart.

It reminded me just how exposed I was. I imagined their eyes roaming my body. Their hands running down their bodies as they watched me get fucked with a fervor they'd never felt before.

"That's the stupidest fucking—" I was cut off with a gasp as they pulled down my shorts before ripping off my stockings and underwear. Their movements were fast, sure. Their fingers pushed through my folds with ease.

This is really happening.

I needed more. Their teasing was driving me insane. I needed them to *take* and take hard.

"*Say it.*"

Their command had my cunt fluttering. My mouth dried up, and it took great effort to swallow against the pressure of their arm on my throat.

"You're so wet. *Achin'*, aren't you?" they asked, their tone more like a purr. "Just say it, and I'll relieve that ache for you."

I'm more than aching. My body was absolutely vibrating with need. The feel of their fingertips against my folds had me quickly turning into the wanton version of myself I showed on the internet.

But this time it's real.

Cam had somehow turned my body into putty, and I was too glad to be used by them.

My hand loosened around the bat, and, just as it was about to fall, Cam grabbed it from me. I whined at the removal of their fingers from my cunt. I had forgotten I even had the bat and cursed myself for not dropping it sooner.

They held it up for me to see.

"We aren't doing this again," they warned. "No more killing. Be a good girl. Listen to me, and I'll reward you. Okay?"

Good girl. I was far from that and had never been called it in my life. There was something so sinful in the way it fell from their lips and felt like more of a curse than a praise.

I clamped my mouth shut to stop whatever noise was about to force itself out. My body wasn't listening to me. It wanted more, and with one wrong move, I would make a fool of myself in front of millions.

A smirk pulled at their lips like they could read every thought that passed through my mind. Like they knew just how much my body wanted to give in, but how my mind wouldn't let it. They put the end of the bat to my neck, trailing it down my body.

"I'm in control here. You can try to fight it, but you won't win. *Now say it.*"

I bucked against them. *I'm not following anything they fucking say. If they think they can control—*

Beep boop.

My inner monologue was interrupted by a tiny beeping. *I know that beep.* We both followed the sound to see a small robot on wheels coming fast toward us, a gift in tow. Same as the one we just encountered, it was large and not too unsimilar to those robot waiters in some of the more gimmicky restaurants.

In the Games, viewers could buy gifts and send them in if they had enough money to spare. The gifts were always three times the price of the outside world, and they were often charged a fee to send them, but if they had enough money, some could even tip the scales in their player's favor.

It would seem my viewers had other ideas, though.

On the after-dark channel, I would get extra money and

sometimes even clothes and purses from loyal viewers. This felt no different.

When the robot got to us, it stopped, and the present popped open. A clear bottle was in the middle, and it was a brand I knew well.

Lube.

"Bubble gum," I breathed, liking where our fans were going with this.

Cam's mouth was on mine in seconds, their hot tongue forcing its way inside while they were still holding me against the wall. They kissed me like they hated me. Like I was truly their ruin, and they wanted me never to forget it.

They kissed me like they wanted to consume me. And I wanted them to.

The bat dropped with a loud clang, and their hand was back between my legs. We weren't that far away from Ella and risked having her hear what was happening.

I hope she does so she knows just how wrapped around my finger Cam is.

Be honest, a voice said at the back of my mind. *It's you who's wrapped around their fingers.*

"Have to get you ready," they murmured between kisses.

Our trackers were going crazy. Ping after ping filled the air, just begging for us to keep it up.

I bit down on her lip *hard.*

They hissed and jerked back at the same time their fingers found my entrance.

There was no gentleness to their movements. No prep with my clit. They forced two fingers inside me and began fucking me like my orgasm was on a time limit.

I threw my head back into the wall, the pain helping push away the fogginess the lack of oxygen had caused as they let up just slightly to allow me a bigger gulp of air. One I took greedily as moans fell from my lips.

The heel of their hand ground against my clit, eliciting curses from me.

They knew what they were doing. Not only that, they were trying to prove me wrong by getting me to my orgasm faster than I had ever experienced.

And it's real.

For the first time since entering the maze, I began to panic. I was going to come. *For real.* In front of millions of people.

One thing I loved about my after-dark channel was the control I had over what the audience saw. And I was damn good at faking my orgasms.

But here was this thembo cowboy, threatening to make me come with just a few strokes of their fingers.

It was downright insulting.

When I jerked against them enough for them to realize their hold on me wasn't as strong as they thought, they switched, replacing their meaty arm with their hand. Their fingers curled around my throat and had me gasping.

I couldn't help the way my body reacted. I was on fire. Whining like a needy cat in heat.

I need more.

"You're gonna be a good girl," they reminded me. Their hand left my cunt to pull at my top, revealing a breast. Their actions were harsh, degrading even, and gave everyone a chance to see me exposed.

Their intake of breath only sent me hurdling closer to my orgasm.

"Touch me," I forced out. "I need to come."

"Not yet. Tell me, Aubrey, do you like havin' everyone watch you come on a stranger's hand?"

Their words had a shocked gasp slipping from my mouth. *Am I that obvious?* My cunt squeezed around nothing, missing the stretch of their fingers.

They didn't give me a chance to respond before their mouth covered my nipple and bit down.

They don't even need to touch me. If they keep doing this, I may just come all on my own.

I couldn't fathom how it was even possible. Even outside my after-dark channel, no one had ever made me come so fast.

Then their hand was gone, and they dropped between my legs.

"Show me that needy pussy."

My hands were pulling up my skirt before I could register that I had actually listened to their command. To make matters worse, I spread my legs for them.

"Good God, you're so sinfully gorgeous." They said it like a curse. "You were made to tempt me."

"Give the people what they want." I was positively shaking with need. My wetness had already begun to pool down my legs, and by the time they were lubing up the handle of the bat, I was panting.

"Have this be your reminder," they said and circled my clit with the bat. It was hard and cold and sent an erotic thrill through me like nothing I had felt before. There were three kills or more on that bat, and they were about to fuck me with it. Punish me in a way that would make me think about it every single time I bashed some Runner's skull in with it.

"Get on with it," I groaned and bucked against them.

"So needy," they murmured and trailed the handle to my entrance.

It was so dirty. So obscene. *And I fucking love every second of it.*

I tried to grind down on it but their hand was at my hips, stopping my movements, reminding me that *they* were the one in control.

Control of my movements. My breathing. *My pleasure.* All of it right in the palm of their hand. They could crush it or nurture it. It all depended on how well I behaved for them.

Slowly, they pushed it into me. The stretch was slightly painful, but so fucking worth it. It was like my pussy was made to take all of it, to take it in greedily, to even beg for more if it fed the hunger in Cam's eyes.

"Give the audience a show, darlin," they said. "This will make you *famous*."

I couldn't respond even if I wanted to because they started fucking me with the bat.

So slow, but so fucking intoxicating. It was dirty, wrong, and there were millions of people watching the handle disappear into my cunt.

"Fuck, you're just sucking it right in," they praised. "Now you're gonna come on this right now and we're gonna move on, you got it?"

I let out a whine and jerked against them. The bat slid into me with little resistance, thanks to their slow movements. They were just getting me used to it, waiting for me to loosen up before—

"Your words, darlin'."

"*Yes*," I breathed. Pleasure threatened to overtake me. The excitement of people watching as I fell apart—for real this time—was overwhelming.

They pulled it back out and slowly pushed it back in, twisting it in a way that made my eyes roll back into my head. They were fucking me faster then. The sickening sound of the bat working through my wet cunt was undeniable and could most definitely be heard through the millions of speakers that were tuned into us.

I all but exploded when her thumb found my clit again. *I can't take it.* Everything was too much. My heart was pounding. My mind was spinning. I couldn't breathe from the sheer force of it.

"Your manners?"

They're fucking pushing it. But I didn't have it in me to fight back. I wanted more. The need to come had my entire body in a vice grip.

"Yes, please!" I all but screamed.

My orgasm was so close, my cunt squeezing the bat so tightly, I was surprised they could even fuck me with it.

But it came, just like they commanded. It swept through me like a tidal wave, its claws digging into my being and threatening to rip me open in front of the world. I seized against the cool wall, letting it overtake me.

The pings were bouncing off the wall like crazy, letting me know our fans loved what we were doing. I could hear their frenzied whispers in my mind, could imagine what they were saying. But even so, I looked at my tracker. I *needed* to see it.

HIDEN'SLUT

Damn, she takes that bat like nobody's business

LIL_MASO_SROKK

She could take more!

LIBRELIBRO23

fuck this year's Games are hotter than ever before

TOTALLYNOTAGAMEMASTER

seriously who allowed straight porn this year?

3_TOAST_BOY_5

show us more tits!

MJS.QUEERBOOKCLUB

put your legs on their shoulders, she looks hungry ;)

They were watching. Not only watching—loving it. It had my pussy clenching tighter than ever. I dropped my hand, my eyes closing as I sunk into the warm feeling that spread across my body.

I was vaguely aware of Cam's soothing words as wave after wave ran through me. It wasn't until I had regained my regular breathing and stopped shaking that they slowly took the bat from me.

I stared down at them, unable to find the words. Their eyes

were narrowed, desire so clear across their face it made me wonder if we'd have another round.

The message from the one fan that suggested I put my legs over their shoulders was starting to sound *very* tempting.

But then, all at once, I was hit with an emotion I rarely felt. *Embarrassment.*

I had just come in front of millions. Cam had plucked it right from my carefully controlled and gridlocked fingers like it was nothing.

"You're lucky I let you even do that," I hissed.

They stood up to their full height, forcing me to tilt my head up to see their face.

They put the bat to my lips, my wetness shining on it.

"Thank me, sugar," they commanded.

Just to spite them, I licked my wetness off the tip. Their eyes flashed dangerously.

"Thank you," I whispered, a feral smile spreading across my lips. This was just the start. I couldn't wait to see what they would do when I got my hands on them.

My hand came to their pants, but they stopped me.

"You're still helping me with my goal, right?"

After that? Fuck yeah, I am.

I nodded.

"And you'll behave? No more killing. And you'll be a good girl and listen to what I say?"

Do they really think I'm going to agree to this?

They gave me a meaningful look, their eyes traveling down my body.

The message was clear: *Be a good girl, and maybe I'll get on my knees for you again.*

I gave them another nod, not trusting my voice to be at full strength again.

"Perfect," they said and put the bat to their mouth before darting out their tongue and dragging it obscenly against the metal. "*Sweet.* Like peaches."

Another violent burst of need shot through me.

They turned away with a smile that lightly graced their lips before I could even comment on their actions.

"You can trust me," I rushed out. "About your goal and the rat."

They paused, looking back at me.

"I know. Better get back on track, peaches."

A warm feeling expanded in my chest. The nickname was a nice touch. Like a secret between the two of us. Only we would know how dirty it was.

I ran my fingers through my curls, unable to keep the smile off my face.

Nothing is going to stop her from getting kicked to the side now.

The rat looked up at us as we walked back, a small frown on their face.

It would have been impossible for her not to have heard it. I wanted her to. Wanted her to know that no matter how hard she tried, Cam would always take my side.

I could see through her game. She might have had them fooled at the beginning, but not me. And I would make sure Cam got to the end of the maze. Even if they didn't agree with my ways.

"Okay, let's get a move on," Cam said and picked up their stuff from the ground.

I stood there, waiting for them to say the magic words... but they never came.

The rat packed up their stuff save for one of the LadyPink bars and ran to catch up to Cam. The flames of anger roared to life as she gave Cam a bar who accepted it with a smile before leading the group forward.

This wasn't the plan!

I stormed after them, catching up to Cam and shooting them a look. One they answered with a small smile instead of actually addressing the elephant in the room.

When I looked back at the rat, she was smiling at me.

Cam

They're called vibes, rat. Get it right.

I was going to hell.

Naw, I wasn't just goin' to hell. I was chasin' hell like the bats that came from it. Failing a test like that? In front of God and everybody?

Ma was going to cuff me so hard around the ears I'd be lucky if I didn't need one of them fancy hearing aids after.

I could still taste her on my lips, the smell of Aubrey washing over my nose and settling onto my taste buds. It was just a tease, allowing myself a delectable morsel of her sweet nectar. But it was enough to get me addicted. I reckoned when this was over and I finally sat that naughty little bitch on my tongue, she wouldn't be getting off for hours.

Well, now that I'd thought about it, maybe not for days, if I had anything to say about it.

The easy glide of the bat through Aubrey's slick center made it difficult to look at the weapon head-on. Well, at least not without considering how easy it'd be to get her onto her back, cursing my name through her clenched teeth. Never met nobody who could look so beautiful while angry as a rattlesnake.

And the way she said my name?

It was hard to care about tests and trials and the paths set out over lifetimes of training when a beautiful woman was purring your name.

If I was off to hell in a handbasket, might as well enjoy the ride.

Ain't nothin' in this world guaranteed, no amount of prayer or offering sure to get me through those gates. But down here? Couldn't I make a bit of my own heaven? Steal a sliver of happiness for myself?

Not like Pa was here to bark at me to do nothin' else. If what he said was even true. I reckoned he believed at least seventy-five percent of it—hard to spend your whole life lying to yourself. But was this really the only way we'd be saved?

Or, like in the maze, was there another path?

There was a chance to be better than the Westons that'd entered the maze before me.

Mercy by an angel whose little pink skirt fluttered with every step she took, offering a glimpse at the tight shorts hugging the curve of her ass. Briefly, I wondered if she was cold without her stockings—long since discarded after I'd ripped them from her body.

The other? Vengeance. That was the name of the game.

Remember your values, what ya were made for. Pa's voice was strong in my head, driving home the family ways I'd already made fools of. Didn't he tell me not to get distracted, not to waste my time with being *nice*? My failures were quickly stacking up, a living reminder walking ahead of me on the path.

And then there was Elijah. He shouldn't't've even been here, and yet there he'd been, standing tall as the day was long with an offering already under his belt.

Why would Pa even send him anyway? It was just another blow below the belt.

The way he'd desecrated a safe zone to appease our holy master? It was perfection. Pretty as a damn peach to see the dull lifeless stare of his victim as we rounded the fountain.

A warning to the rest of the Runners that there was a predator amidst the flock of sheep.

And he had that damned Architect, Hiram, too. Elijah was too smart for his own fucking good.

It made a person think, my choice to take the path less traveled by the Westons—peace—weighing on me, heavy as a bunch of bricks.

But this was my show, my chance to prove myself to Pa and get out for good.

My fingernails bit into my palm where my fists clenched at my sides, jaw tense.

Didn't they trust me to get the job done? To bring home the win?

With the way you behave? Pa's voice sneered. *You still have time to fix this. Kill the girls, make a show of it. Prove that there is nothing more important to you than the glory and power of your God. Show the world your devotion. You still have time, Camil—*

"Fuck off, I can do this my way," I hissed at the demon lurking in my mind, the sound of my own furious voice bringing me back to the real world.

"What?" Ella asked, looking over her shoulder at me, her fingers still lightly tracking the wall as she walked.

Aubrey paused, shooting me a look that warned she was angry as a wasp's nest that I hadn't sent Ella off. Clearly she was still too furious to bother talkin' to me. But what did she expect me to do?

Drop Ella just because I'd made her come?

Okay, yeah, that's *exactly* what she'd expected me to do.

It was... sorta cute. The way she stomped around mad as a wet cat.

Even though she was pissed, her hand slid over mine to pry it open, threadin' our fingers together to lead me down the corridor just behind Ella. Sparks licked at the places where our skin met.

At first glance, she didn't seem like the sinful temptation she truly was. She really looked like an angel, even if she just so happened to be a blood-streaked one.

Or maybe a doll. Her golden hair swaying with every step. That perfect body that looked like it was modeled just for me.

It was hard to forget just how well my hands fit on her hips. How readily she opened up for me.

The thrill from what we'd done lingered as we continued our path. The image of her face twisted in pleasure and the sounds of her delicious whines playin' over and over again in my mind like a record.

I can't wait to watch the video when I get out of here.

I'd been spitting mad—still was, if I was being honest—about how she'd murdered those Runners. I told her from the beginnin' I wasn't no player killer. That I didn't wanna be like my family. Wanted to win the game my way.

It was her fault that the darkness was threatenin' to overtake me, to pull me back into the depths of the nearsighted thinking my parents had tried to instill in me from birth. I'd fought every instinct to be better, to treat others with kindness. But with her, all of that went out the window.

Aubrey'd gone crazy, barrelin' into the people with the metal bat like it was a fuckin' game. Her face splattered with blood, twisted in her anger. An angel of vengeance amidst her public. There was a part of me that called for her. That enjoyed every moment of it.

She would make a show of it.

Did it make me sick that I longed for it? I knew I didn't want to be like them, the monsters who'd raised me to treat human life like it was another piece in a chess game. But the feeling I'd had watching cute, innocent-looking Aubrey in her sparkly pink clothes brutally murderin' Runners... It was nothing less than feral lust.

A need for her that threatened to overtake my good sense.

It had to be a test. The way the darkness loomed over me, threatening to smother my good intentions and drag me back into the light. My glory was whispered. Promised. *My salvation.*

I thought I had it under control. Thought I could push the urges to the back of my mind, even just for the sake of winning.

Aubrey, though... She made me feel things I shouldn't.

She made me *do* things I shouldn't.

I shouldn't have wanted to watch as her cunt swallowed a bat splattered with her victims' blood. My mouth shouldn't have watered when her pink tongue flicked out to lick her own cum off it. Shouldn't have gotten off to watching her almost come while choking her out.

My cunt ached from the memory, my own needs going unanswered a hollow offering in the name of my quickly deteriorating sanity.

More than everything, I sure as fuck shouldn't want to ditch Ella just to see what deplorable things Aubrey would do to show her gratitude.

But I did.

I didn't have time to think through what that meant for the state of my mental health. Though I reckoned the dull, gray, never-ending concrete walls of the maze would make me go insane far faster than my own twisted libido.

We paused as we came up to a section with several doors. More doors than people in our group.

Another fucking choice.

I glanced at my watch, nothing useful coming from the quickly moving messages in the chat. It was hard to tell if that was because we were the first to come up to this particular obstacle or if they really were just that feral to see me fuck Aubrey into the next dimension.

AMZYFIELDER

I found her afterdark channel! GET THE COWBOY ON THERE

AUTHORBEXDEVEAU

FUCK !! THE!! BLONDE!!

LIL_MASO_SROKK

I'd pay hella cash to see that performance
again in 4k

Exhaustion was beginning to weigh on me. Without the sun, it was hard to gauge how much time had passed, but given we'd already made it through the halfway point... I had to guess it'd been at least three hours, if not four.

Either way, my body was beginning to feel the effects of constant spikes of adrenaline. I'd long since used up the quick carbs I'd eaten at breakfast with all the heavy lifting I'd done getting my ass out of stupid situations—and supporting my teammates. Even the protein bar I had wasn't helping. The physical drain of the maze was obvious on all three of us the moment jogging had turned into walking.

And there was still a lot to go.

The voice inside my head that sounded like Pa kept hissin' at me to leave them, reminding me that they were just holding me back.

You could kill 'em. Two less Runners to compete with. Remember your goal.

But there was no way I could bring myself to do it. I couldn't imagine hurtin' Aubrey, much less killin' her.

A part of me wanted her to look up at me in fear as I chased her down, but that feat should be twinged with excitement for all the different ways I wanted to ravage her.

Not because I was going to kill her.

"Which way?" Aubrey asked, looking up at me. Her voice making the fog in my mind clear, if even for just a moment.

A bit of her lipstick was smudged on the side of her mouth, the only evidence of what we had done besides her missing panties.

My hand twitched, the urge to smear it even more too strong.

Fuck. Get a grip, Cam.

To distract myself, I looked down at my tracker. Comments

were up in the millions, and my viewership still in the hundreds of thousands. As it fuckin' should be after a show like that.

> AMZYFIELDER
>
> Can we get back to the sex?
>
> HIDEN'SLUT
>
> Ditch the add-on and show us more of that pretty little thing's cunt.
>
> AUTHORBEXDEVEAU
>
> +1
>
> AUTHORJASMINEGARCIA
>
> I wanna see her on her knees for you! I'll send you a vibrator if you do!
>
> AUTHORBEXDEVEAU
>
> +1000

"We could each take one?" Ella suggested. "Go in a bit and come back to report our findings."

I opened my mouth to reply, but Aubrey was faster. "Great idea. You take any of them, and Cam and I will take a different one."

"I meant that we'd each take our own door," Ella said, her brows pulling together in confusion.

"I know what you meant," Aubrey answered flatly. "What I meant was that it's time for you to get lost."

I squeezed her hand, frowning. "Peaches, we talked about this."

"No, you talked, and I pretended to agree to get to the good stuff. Can't you see that she's slowing us down? And this stupid bitch nearly got you killed back in that stupid fucking fountain. I'm so fucking sick of—"

"Only PKer here is you, Aubrey," Ella interrupted hotly, glaring at the blonde. "Don't think I didn't catch all those red lights."

"And what about it? They would've happily killed you too!

Just as a reminder, you stupid bitch, if anything, I saved your life. You should be thanking me instead of giving this high-and-fucking-mighty lecture." Ella rolled her eyes and flicked her hair over her shoulder. "You chose to be here like the rest of us, leech."

Her viciousness had my stomach flipping.

She's talking back again, the voice in my head warned. *Making trouble.*

The last lesson hadn't been enough.

Next time, I'd have to be more thorough.

There was a pause, Ella's dark eyes shifting to me before she huffed, then asked, "Do you want me gone?"

"W-what—?" I spluttered, shakin' my head to clear the filthy image of Aubrey bent over my knee, screamin' for me to stop as I struck her reddened bottom. "No, I think we need to stick together at this point... Things are gonna get more difficult now. The midpoint ain't the time to turn on each other." I said the last bit mostly for Aubrey's benefit, my voice holdin' a sharp edge.

I was startin' to think Aubrey'd never watched this event before. We could shove Ella behind us and step onto the podium together... but PKing a teammate? Splitting up and letting Ella potentially get ahead on a few lucky turns? Fuck that. This was *our* game.

There was no way I was going to let a player I'd carried this far beat me because the girl I liked was jealous. Peaches was just going to have to fuckin' deal, and I'd show her the consequences after.

Aubrey rolled her eyes, Ella meetin' her with a furious scowl. The two of them were angier than a couple cats in a pillowcase, but we *really* didn't have time for no more bickerin'.

"You know—" Ella started, lip curled in disgust as she looked down her nose at Aubrey, the blonde reactin' immediately by movin' towards her.

"Enough," I said, puttin' a hand out to catch Aubrey. "We need to pick a door." My tone didn't hold room to arguin', forcing Ella into silence.

And thank fuck for that, I was gettin' tired of her voice.

With a glance at my watch, I could see from the compass we were pointing northwest, neither of the doors giving any real hint as to what direction they would ultimately lead or what fresh fucking horrors we'd find inside.

Totally unassuming.

I was one step away from either winning this thing or sending myself to an early grave.

A more bloodthirsty player would make their companions go first, only to follow after they were sure it was safe. It was true I didn't want to kill Ella outright, but I also didn't have much of an urge to protect her either.

But Aubrey?

"Go on, Peaches," I murmured, nudging Aubrey's shoulder. "Take a pick."

I was just as likely to save her life as I was my own.

"Only 'cause you asked so nicely," she said, offering a flirty little wink before turning her attention back to the doors.

"We're fucking doomed," Ella muttered under her breath. "She'll probably pick it on feeling alone."

"They're called vibes, rat. Get it right," Aubrey snarked, rolling her eyes. "Besides, you always go left, right?" She turned to look at me for confirmation.

"Perceptive. Good girl," I praised, not even trying to smother my smile.

Ella let out an offended scoff, her bare arms crossing over her chest.

Aubrey reached a manicured hand forward, grasping onto the doorknob on the leftmost side and turning. She pushed the door open to total and complete darkness. I'd expected the same plain gray walls and low light of the rest of the maze, but the blackness beyond the doorframe was a bit jarring in contrast.

The three of us waited, a second passing by with nothing but squeaking meeting our ears.

No trap?

Vibes. Right. Okay. Not at all what I had trained my entire fucking life for, but sure, whatever worked. I could get with it.

I took a step closer, tryin' to get my eyes to adapt to the darkness beyond.

At first, I reckoned the ground beyond was uneven, the unlit corridor seeming to sway with movement. That was until hundreds of pairs of little red eyes turned toward the light at once, a swarm of rats moving in unison to lunge for the door like some sort of combined force.

Aubrey screamed, falling backwards with the clatter of her baseball bat hitting the stone before she could try to slam the door shut, forcing Ella and me into action, my hand catching the door just as the first of the creatures began to cross the threshold.

Ella grabbed Aubrey by her arms, hauling her backwards as I struggled with the door, but it was no use. The rats quickly overtook me, climbin' up my boots and aimin' to sink their sharp fangs into my skin like a hearty gouda. I knew that sometimes they brought things into the Games that defied the laws of nature and science, but this was the first time I'd seen it myself. Incredibly fast, strong, and totally mindless, save for the resolve to devour whatever was closest to them, the rats were quick to go after the other girls.

Aubrey scrambled to her feet, her bat lost to the swarm, leaving her with only her platformed boots to stomp hard on heads in an attempt to try and stop them from reaching her skin.

I shook the creatures off the best I could, wading through the veritable sea of rodents for the next door.

"Run to me!" I barked at Aubrey and Ella, bracing my hand on the doorknob. "When I count to three!"

Ella shrieked, throwing one of the rats down the hall. "Three!" she shouted, sprinting for the door. Aubrey looked at her with a glare, her hands reaching out and tangling in the girl's hair in an attempt to pull her back.

"Let go!"

"This is your sign to get the fuck out of here, cunt," Aubrey growled and shoved herself in front of the girl. But Ella was right behind, determined not to be left alone with the murderous swarm of rodents.

I swung the door open just as the girls reached me, the three of us tumbling into the darkness beyond as I slammed it shut behind us.

Aubrey panted hard from somewhere nearby, and I reached for her blindly while my eyes began to adjust to the sudden black.

"Should've fucking left her," Aubrey said between huffs.

"Bitch, do you ever let up?" Ella asked, venom laced in her tone. "I saved your pathetic ass, and this is how you—"

"I'll fucking shut you up, you—"

"Enough," I hissed. "Both of you." Silence followed my command.

Good girl. The phrase was on the tip of my tongue. I forced myself to swallow it. She didn't need any more encouragement from me.

Ella lit the face of her watch, shining the tiny screen around the room in an effort for us to get our bearings and understand where we were and how we were meant to get out.

Aubrey did the same, but instead of lookin' at the floors or walls for some way out, she was looking at me, her filthy, blood-streaked face pinched with concern.

"You're okay?" she asked softly, reaching out to touch one of the many scratches and bites crisscrossing my arms.

For a moment, I had seen real fear on her face back in the corridor.

And I fuckin' hated it.

I never wanted to see it again. It had a grip on my heart. The only fear or panic I ever wanted the blonde bombshell to feel was because of me, not some fucked-up Architect who thought sendin' mutant rats after us was funny.

"Yeah, darlin', I'm all good," I murmured, catching her hand in mine and bringing it to my lips for a brush against her knuckles. "You? That was pretty scary, huh?"

She sniffed, nodding. "I fucking hate rats."

Aubrey didn't seem so much like sin right now. The tremble in her voice was convincin', but I reckoned tests were supposed to be like this.

Difficult to pass. Concealing themselves as something innocent when in reality they were the world's greatest sin.

It made it so much harder.

I moved to pull her to me, lookin' to give a bit of comfort, when Ella scoffed behind us.

"If you're quite done, I think I've found the way out."

Aubrey made an irritated little noise like a rattlesnake.

"We should've left you out there," she sniped, hand firmly lockin' with mine as she towed me toward the spot in the wall Ella was shinin' her watch on. "But at least you have *some* use."

I wanted to sigh. I didn't know what was more exhausting— the maze or their annoying-ass feud.

"You are such an ungrateful bitch, you know?" Ella said flatly. "Any ideas on how to solve this?"

Using my own watch, I added to the light, looking at the pipes embedded into the wall. They were mismatched, the water trying to get in from the ceiling splatterin' down onto the floor.

Jesus fuck, was I sick of being wet.

I worked backwards, looking for the answer to the puzzle. "I reckon the water needs to get to the pipe at the bottom..." I muttered. "So we'll need to... move it around?"

Aubrey was looking at the pipes, her mind trying to work through the puzzle. "At least it isn't fucking blood this time," she grumbled.

"Blood?" Ella asked.

"You don't wanna know," I said. "Reeked worse than the pig pen in 109-degree heat."

The brunette shivered. "Fair enough. You think we're getting close to the end?"

"Must be." It was more hopeful than anything, but I moved my wrist to look at my watch all the same.

The viewer count was still good. In the hundreds of thousands. The comments on the other hand...

MJS.QUEERBOOKCLUB

God this is so BORING!! Fuck the girls already! No one gives a shit about making it out.

ELLEMAEBOOKS

Typing this with one hand ;) ready for anything

LIBRELIBRO23

Weston4ever! I'd like the next turn to ride the cowboy 315-XXX-XXX

This is what I fucking get for letting my desires get the best of me. The audience didn't care about me winning. All they wanted was to see me fucking Aubrey again.

The temptation was there again, teasing the edges of my mind and setting my body alight.

But as I scrolled I saw more positive ones.

3_TOAST_BOY_5

Try turning the top left two!

BOOKBOUDOIRYEG

The middles can make an "L" shape if you turn the right one!

I cleared my throat, ready to share the ideas with the team. "Seems like some people–"

"Hey!" shouted, her voice bouncing off the walls. "I need that!"

Aubrey

Is this what death felt like?

If Cam wasn't so... *Cam,* I would've already bashed that bitch's head in.

I scrambled after Ella, staring at my watch in her hand as she moved to cozy up beside Cam to look at the walls. How the fuck she'd managed to get it so expertly off my wrist was anyone's guess. She leaned closer to the pipes, using the light from my stolen watch to inspect each of them.

The water dripped from my skin in icy droplets, freezing my insides and slowing my movements. In the short time we'd been in the room, the chill had gotten so bad my fingers began to numb.

First they wanted to boil us, then they wanted to freeze us. What else? Is a fiery pit waiting to swallow us up? Spikes? Flesh-eating bugs?

"Shouldn't be that hard, if you aren't a bimbo Barbie at least," Ella muttered, her free hand already pulling at the pipes, trying to match up the like sides.

"Aw, baby, I'd rather be bimbo Barbie than stuck as forget-table *stupid* Skipper," I hissed, reaching to grab my watch from her hand.

She shot me a look. I shot her one back before my stiff fingers closed around the watch, pulling it from her grasp and reattaching it to my wrist. It was pinging like crazy, but I was too focused on the rat to even consider looking at the flood of messages.

"Do you want to get out of here or not? We don't have time for you to fuck around with the goddamn puzzle."

"Quit touchin' shit," Cam said with an irritated sigh. "Last time you did it didn't end so nice. Haven't you learned fuckin' anythin' in here? If we just take our time and work *together*—"

"You should've shut the fucking door on her," I said, stepping closer to Ella with a sneer. "You're not just holding us back, you're a fucking *liability*. Cam may not be able to see it, but I see right fucking through you."

Ella rolled her eyes and turned back to the wall of pipes.

"Whatever," she mumbled under her breath. "You might not see it, but I care about Cam. We're *friends*. And you might have some kind of weirdo obsession with them, but that doesn't change anything. I'm getting the fuck out of here—"

A loud *click* echoed through the room as Ella moved one of the pipes with a triumphant shout.

"*See*? I told you I could figure this shit out—"

"Fuckin' *shit*—"

It happened so fast there was no way to brace for it.

There was no sound. No rumbling. Not even the telltale tingling sensation that something was wrong.

One moment we were standing in the dark, water raining down on us in a slow, cold drizzle, and the next, the floor beneath us was open. Slanted toward a pitch-black gap in the center of the room.

"Fuck!"

I scrambled to hold on to the wall, my fingers slipping off the slick pipes as gravity failed me. The floor was at a heavy angle, my nails digging into the rough, wet surface of the jagged ground in an effort to stop myself from falling.

Hot pain shot up my hands and arms, adrenaline the only thing warming my body as ice-cold fear overtook me.

Ella's scream echoed up to us as she rocketed downward, a loud splash following.

"Christ on a cracker," Cam swore from their place at my side. They were trying to hold on as well, but there was no use. The floor was too tilted, the ground too wet. Booted feet slipping as we couldn't find purchase. "Sorry, Peaches," they groaned, sliding off the shallow lip and tumbling into darkness.

I didn't have time to worry—or worse, to *mourn*. I had to hope that the initial splash I'd heard from Ella's fall meant there was enough water at the bottom of the pit to stop them from breaking bones. But then there was the concern of whatever might be in the water with them.

"Fuck this," I growled and tried to use my boot to force my body up again. My nails were screaming at me to stop. My body was shaking with the force it took to keep me up.

But just like Cam, it was no use. My body gave up.

Splash.

My boot slipped, and with it went the rest of my grip. I fell down into the blackness. My back hit the edge of the tunnel I was thrown into, knocking the air from my lungs. I gasped. My hands outstretched feebly to grab on to something—*anything*—as I fell down.

Is this what death felt like?

The unending, potent fear that gripped my entire body? Did everyone feel this way?

The hole had to lead somewhere. And if I was falling down, and fast, that meant my untimely end would be there at the end waiting for me.

For a moment, it was a bit like how I'd imagined flying to be. Weightless, almost magical in its suspension from reality.

This wasn't like being thrown during cheer practice. This was something else.

Something *more*.

Ella's screams stopped when she hit the water, the only sound in my ears now the whooshing of the wind as I fell. The sound was like music to my ears. But any joy that was brought by it was smashed by hearing Cam fall through the air and hit the ground.

It hurt more than expected. The knowledge that they were hurt. The fear that they were seriously injured even more so.

Was it worth it? A small voice whispered in the back of my mind. *You're gonna end up just like Natalie. Dying a boring, unsatisfying death. Just because you wanted to prove something to the world.*

I hated that voice. Hated how it attacked my being. Hated how the same overcritical thing, far too close to my grandmother's voice, showed me picture after picture of my unsatisfactory life over and over again as I fell.

I didn't want to listen to it.

I wouldn't.

"Fuck you—"

Pain. Mind-blowing, sharp pain flashed through my body as my back hit water and then, far too quickly, the ground.

Cam

Turned out that no matter how many vitamins you took or perfectly balanced meals designed for performance you ate, a twenty-five-foot free fall into a foot and a half of water still hurt like a fuckin' bitch.

Goddamn, I'm fucking sick of being wet, I thought again.

I didn't remember so much water in previous years. Though, maybe I was just unlucky, you know?

Or maybe I was just making the wrong choices, and this was my punishment. A warning that I was close to losing the Games. *And my life.* A little tidbit that became abundantly clear as I sat up, rubbing my side irritably.

My body throbbed, my lungs aching with each inhale.

And I fucking reek. There was too much blood. Too much water that'd dried on me.

Like a horse taken out for a hard ride and put back wet.

I'm so fucking done with this.

None of my siblings' Games seemed to be such a disgrace. Such an embarrassment. It was like the Architects went out of their way to degrade the Runners in every way possible.

Maybe they were low on funding.

They're just better than you, Pa's voice whispered in my mind.

You're a disappointment. Can't even get to the end of the Games, let alone make a solid offering.

"Enough," I whispered, anger making it hard to think straight. "*Fucking enough.*"

My mind was spinning, trying to come to terms with the fall, almost dying, and the nagging thought that because I wasn't doing good enough, I was a failure to my family. *To my God.*

No offering. No winning. No vengeance. No offering. No winning. No vengeance.

My head was pounding with each word echoing through my mind.

Failure. No offering. Failure. No winning. Disappointment. No vengeance.

Again. Again. And again.

No winning. Disappointment. No vengeance. Fail—

A loud moan of pain sounded throughout the room, echoing off the wall.

Relief hit me like a tractor.

Right. I wasn't alone. I had my very own crazy guardian angel coming to my ruin.

And thank God for that.

"Aubrey?" I called, listening to the blonde wheeze a few feet away while watching as Ella sat up, coughing water.

"I am so fucking sick of you idiots," she groaned, crawling on hand and knee for the lip of the shallow pool, hauling herself out.

A bit rude, but I guessed I could see how it seemed like her misfortune was our mistake.

The Architects are trying to kill us.

Not only did they set off a fucking tsunami in a closed maze, but they had us free falling to a concrete floor below with only very little water to soften our fall.

I'd prepared for damn near anything, but somehow, after years of Games, they managed to surprise me.

At least there weren't no spikes waitin'.

Didn't much care for becoming a kebab.

"It's your fault, you cunt," Aubrey said with a groan.

I followed after Ella, the sound of water sloshing behind me warning that Aubrey was starting to fight her way to the lip herself.

"At least I'm *trying*!" Ella said, sending a venomous glare toward Aubrey. "You're just a fucking leech, not even contributing anything to getting us the fuck out of here. All you do is mess things up, whine about not getting that fucked-up cowboy's attention, and whore yourself out for the entire world to see! Don't think I didn't hear your disgusting begging for Cam to fuck you!"

Fuck that. Aubrey was rash and had a questionable moral code, but I wouldn't stand by and watch as Ella talked to her like that.

"Watch it," I warned the brunette. "Don't you be gettin' ugly on her. We could've just left you back there with the rats."

"Told you she's a cunt," Aubrey said, rocketing blood out of her nose. "Leave. I told your dumb ass we don't need you."

Ella got strangely quiet after that. I should have taken it as the red flag that it was.

I hauled myself out of the shallow pool, turning to offer Aubrey a hand up when the unmistakable cool press of metal against my back made me freeze.

*No way. No **fucking** way.*

Aubrey'd been right. The entire fucking time.

I'm a goddamn fool.

I wanted to believe that Ella was good. Didn't wanna be like my siblings, so I actively ignored the voice in the back of my mind that told me to ditch her—to kill her.

And look where that fuckin' got me.

On the business end of a knife *I'd* stolen. I thought I was able to nick it undetected from Elijah's goon but someone saw it. *Ella.* She'd seen everything and had been slowly planning her move.

Mother. Fucker.

Ella shifted behind me, pushing the sharp end of the knife into my back hard enough to send a burst of pain through me.

It was high up, between one of my ribs... and right where my lungs were.

It would kill me. *She's trying to kill me.*

Anger. Betrayal. Anxiety. All of it exploded inside me. My skin itched with it. My hands shook. I couldn't wrap my head around it. Couldn't believe—

How fuckin' stupid you are. It was Pa's voice again. This time I didn't tell him to shut up. He was just whispering my own thoughts back to me.

I watched in slow motion as Aubrey moved closer to us, oblivious to the shift in power. The annoyingness on her features hadn't yet changed to rage. Those sharp eyes of hers had yet to home in on Ella.

I had but mere seconds until she came to the same conclusion I did.

It was one thing for her to stab me in the back, but...

I didn't know what I was more worried about. Ella hurting Aubrey, or what Aubrey would try to do to the girl once she found out she had a knife to my back.

"Peaches, stay right there," I called, putting my hand up to stop Aubrey from advancing.

Maybe this is the test. Maybe it's not Aubrey at all.

It's Ella.

I hadn't once suspected her. Not even when Aubrey had so unabashedly called her out on it. Because, in my mind, the temptation of Aubrey should have been the sin. That was the easiest to pinpoint.

But that was the whole point of a test. And I had almost failed it.

Almost.

The whole time in the maze, God had been showing me flashes. Reminding me of what I needed to do. And I ignored it. But now His message was clear.

Make a show of it.

And fuck me, I was ready to spit venom. Making a show was the least I'd do.

I still had a chance. And I wasn't going to let it slip through my fingers.

Aubrey rolled her eyes, continuing her path toward us, my heart beating a thousand miles an hour in my chest with every waterlogged step.

Now it was a game of who could move the fastest.

If Ella did, and punctured a vital organ, I wasn't entirely sure I'd manage to survive long enough to crack her skull open.

A sort of wave washed over me, pushing away all my fears and worries about Aubrey.

She was never the test.

I almost felt... giddy.

Like the knowledge of that alone would be enough to push me to do what I needed to.

Now, I was a good old-fashioned southerner, and when I needed to apologize to my girl, it was customary to bring a gift. Usually, I would've opted for flowers, maybe something sparkly to take the edge off. Aubrey was just going to have to make do with what I had on hand—the severed hand of her enemy.

If ya bite the hand that fuckin' feeds ya, expect them to take yours clean off.

God gave me a hell of a reminder of who I was, and I was keen to make good on it. Now that I *knew* I could have her, my little bloodied angel, I sure as shit wasn't going to let no traitorous little witch take her from me.

"One more step," Ella called. "And I'll run them through with this knife. You think taking out a Weston will give me a nice final score boost? Only one way to find out, right?"

My watch buzzed on my wrist, not that I had an opportunity to look at the messages... Or that I could deal to see what Hope had to say about the damned predicament that I'd gotten myself into.

Fuckin' embarassin'.

"Slowly take a step and turn to your left," Ella commanded. When I didn't move right away, she pushed the sharp tip of the knife deeper into my skin.

With a sigh, I did as ordered. Didn't much like being walked around like a dog, but there was nothing to be done about it for the moment.

"You see those chains?" she asked. My eyes caught two shiny chains on either side of a grate that separated us from the rest of the maze. "You're coming with me."

"Don't," Aubrey said, her eyes moving between me and Ella, rounded with worry.

My perfect little angel coming to the rescue.

I didn't know it was possible to fall so madly in love with someone so quickly, but a little temptation had turned into a full-blown *craving* for her.

A craving to take her. A craving to destroy her. A craving to ruin her in ways that would make the good Lord shy away in fear. And knowin' Aubrey, she'd gladly take anything I was fixin' to give her.

I reckon it won't be without no fight, but that's the fun of it.

Aubrey's lips parted, hand twitching at her side for a baseball bat that I was sure she was sorely missing now that I was in a world of trouble.

"Ella, c'mon, let's talk about this," I said smoothly, turning my head to look at her out of the corner of my eye with one of those charming, lopsided smiles.

The girl I'd called an ally was all but gone, her face twisted and cruel as her darkened eyes bore up into mine.

The plan was already forming before she replied.

"Oh, fuck off, Weston. That shit isn't going to work on me now."

Make a show of it, Pa's voice said, back and stronger than ever. It was ringing in my head, sounding strangely like the church bells back home that rang whenever a good little worshiper did God's deeds.

They will ring for me too. I'll make sure of it.

"I will," I whispered back.

"What did you say?" Ella asked, twisting the knife. I let out a pained hiss.

"Nothin'," I replied through gritted teeth.

She paused before speaking again, her distrust hanging heavy in the air. "Walk, Cam. You're going to help me open the door."

I nodded, not like I had much choice, and walked on leaden feet toward the metal gate on the far side of the room.

Water sloshed behind us, and the knife pressed further into my back, making me wheeze.

"Aubrey!" I barked. "Stay."

Not a request. An order to an unruly puppy too eager to follow its master.

I pulled one side of the chain, and Ella did the same, the metal grating sliding down into the floor, opening up the corridor beyond.

"Go on," Ella sneered. "In you go."

Idiot. The last thing you want to do is make it so that I don't have to worry about Aubrey's safety if things go south from my trying to attack you.

It's too good. Too perfect.

God was guidin' me.

I stepped through, Ella turning to look at Aubrey through the grate.

"Don't worry, *Peaches*," she sneered back at Aubrey. "I'll take good care of your little cowboy."

Aubrey's furious glare shoulda peeled paint. I could practically see the bloodthirsty thoughts swirling around her head.

I hope she loves what I'm gonna do. It's a present for both God and my bloodied angel.

Ella didn't stay long after the grate closed, shoving us along the corridor quickly.

It wouldn't be long until Aubrey caught up with us.

Ella looked at her watch, a filthy smirk crossing her features as she stopped, shoving her hand into a hole in the wall and pulling hard on a lever I hadn't noticed hidden inside.

The floor rumbled, the stone walls around us beginning to rise and lower, the once long hall in front of us shortening into a dead end as the wall to our left opened wide. Dust and debris showered down on us, the ground unsteady at our feet as the maze rotated.

The fucking bitch was resetting the game.

AUBREY

I'LL SEE YOU ON THE OUTSIDE.

I *fucking knew that bitch was up to something!* Should've trusted my gut and killed her as soon as I'd seen that stupid water bottle touch her lips. Thirsty? As if. I'd watched enough K-dramas in my day to know an indirect kiss when I saw one.

Fucking. Bullshit.

I'd tried to warn Cam, tried to tell them that she was a no-good snake, but damn, they just did not want to believe that Ella was someone trying to actively harm them. The annoying bitch played off the ditzy bimbo shtick even better than I did.

And now this.

I heard it before I saw it. The freeze in the surrounding air. The intake of breath from Cam. Fuck, I could even taste their rage.

My eyes were still glued to the silvery blade pressed against Cam's back as they stood locked in place beside their should-be friend. This entire time, she had been sneakily waiting for her chance to take us down.

And now she has it.

Maybe she had enough of us almost dying and wanted to end things herself. People do crazy things for money.

I didn't know what she wanted the prize money for, or why she entered the Games. But she was the weakest type of Runner.

Yet the most conniving.

I should've killed her when I had the chance, I thought savagely, taking a chance at another small step forward—anything that would get me closer to them. In range to *actually* help.

Not that I was sure how I was going to do that, exactly. But I needed to think of *something.* I had never before felt panic the way I did when Cam was threatened.

I've always been the person that got things done. Everything was *always* under my control. I was able to do anything. *Be* anything. And I never even had to think about it.

But her taking Cam away washed every ounce of confidence I had from me.

The urge to act was so strong it overpowered me in a way I never expected.

My feet froze in place as Ella reached into the wall, panic killing my voice in my throat.

A trap?! What kind of coward uses a trap to kill somebody instead of doing it themselves?

There was a low, grumbling rumble, the floor under my feet quaking and making the water from the shallow pool lap against the stony edge. Shaking hard enough that I lost my balance, stumbling forward and having to catch myself on my hands, scraping them on the rough ground.

The world slowed down around me as my panic became horror. She wasn't trying to kill Cam with a trap at all.

She was separating us.

The walls all around us began to move and change, cracking in half before burrowing up into the ceiling. To my right and left, where there were once dead ends, long hallways opened, offering a view into new areas—and revealing Runners whose faces matched my own confusion and horror as they attempted to dodge walls and new obstacles.

The thoughts came in quick succession.

The maze is resetting.

If we aren't careful, she'll crush us.

Fuck, I didn't realize anyone had managed to catch up.

I pushed myself back up, using the force to propel myself forward toward the grate as the metal bars began to move toward the ceiling again, blocking me from entering the hall. My body made contact with the solid grate, cursing loudly as I reached an arm through the bars.

The coldness and pain from the earlier rooms hit me like a truck. It stifled my movements. Had my hands shaking.

Cam was *so* close, Ella at their back with the tip of the knife poised upwards, the pair of them watching as I struggled to get the stupid grate to move. Not that any of the rattling I was doing did any fucking good.

"Aubrey, babygirl, it's okay," Cam said tightly, taking in a sharp breath as the knife pricked in deeper. "I'll see you on the outside."

Their face was pinched, anxious, but their voice? All luxuriously calm. Even in a situation like this, they were looking out for others—for me.

Why?

I'd expected to see the sharp-nosed little fuckhead beside them smiling, gloating that she'd managed to pull one over on us. But the rat wasn't smiling. If anything, she looked worried—maybe even a bit fearful.

Good, I thought savagely. *She fucking should be.*

I was going to tear her fucking head off.

Starting by ripping out those ugly, ratty extensions she was trying to pass off as her own hair. There was a reason I wouldn't let the half-cracked stylists they'd hired touch me.

"If you hurt them," I called to Ella, making her pale, blotchy face lose even more color. "I'll make sure you wish you'd never been born!"

She gasped softly, tongue snaking out to lick her lips anxiously. It was nice to know my threats still had some weight despite me looking like a drowned rat. Like Ella was panicking even though she was the one with the upper hand.

The girl who was taking Cam away from *me*.

Running in my heavy, clunky platforms was a sport in and of itself, but *nothing* was going to stop me from going after that bitch. *Nobody* touched what belonged to me.

"You bitch! You think I'll stop when you're dead?!"

The words that were racing through my head were spilling from my lips before I could stop them.

"I'll cut that pretty hair off! Slit your throat! Smash your head in! You're parents won't even recgonize the mush of bone and flesh they drop at their doorstep!"

My anger and bloodthirst were renewed, all of the venom and spite I'd reserved for Natalie finding a new target in Ella. I saw images of her violent death flashing across my mind over and over again. Oh, what I wouldn't have given in that moment for my bat to crush her useless, conniving skull in.

Cam watched with wide eyes, the reality of their situation *finally* dawning on them—that their *bestie* was going to kill them. And there was nothing that either of us could do about it.

The rest of the hallway was sealed with a stone wall, cutting off my view of Cam, and I jerked into motion, my boots pounding against the concrete beneath my feet as I threw myself into the closest tunnel, trying to follow it to get as close to them as I could.

My heart was racing in my chest, the adrenaline pumping straight into my veins—but that wasn't the only thing pushing me forward. Forcing me to ignore the aches and pains of the drop or the discomfort of my blistered heels.

Excitement licked through me, accompanied by its favorite companion—*rage.*

Excitement because I'd *finally* be able to kill her. This time I knew Cam wouldn't try and stop me. Not now that they'd seen her for exactly what she was—a dirty, scheming rat. A fucked-up leech with no shot of winning the Games on her own that'd attached herself to a much bigger, more effective predator.

And rage... It made my eyes prick with bitter, overly salinized tears. How fucking dare she try to kill them? Cam's life was *mine* —*they were mine*—and I liked them exactly the way they were, thank you very much.

And then there was something else... Something hard to identify. An emotion that had me sick to my stomach and my heart aching.

It hurt. Knowing that they could be in real trouble.

I hadn't known them for long but in the time I did, they burrowed themselves inside me. Akin to a parasite. They changed my thoughts. Twisting them until they were all about them. Until I longed to always be next to them. Until I felt real fear and panic at the loss of their presence.

The ground jerked under me, slowing my progress as I slipped. My eyes fell to the stones where they'd cracked, shooting across the space between me and the next corridor.

I screamed in frustration, jumping up onto the rapidly rising bit of stone, only to realize that the ceiling was also beginning to descend. I needed to move fast if I wanted to avoid being crushed to death.

"Aubrey!" Cam's anxious voice cut through the buzzing in my ears as I scrambled over the stonework, barely rolling over the lip and onto the other side before the two pieces connected with an angry grinding noise that let me know I was very nearly just made into an extremely good-looking pancake.

I righted myself, brushing some pebbles from my scratched-up knee, just in time to watch another set of walls begin to close.

Fear.

Cam was on the other side of the descending walls, and at the rate they were moving... I wouldn't make it.

All thoughts of killing the rat left my mind. *Killing can wait, I need to get to her.*

I jerked into motion, but I was too slow.

The walls slammed together, and the last thing I saw was Cam's shocked face as Ella approached them from behind, the knife clutched in her trembling hand.

I slammed my fist on the wall once, twice, a third time, and hard enough to draw blood.

"Cam! I'm coming! *Cam!*"

I could hear something from the other side, but it was no use. The stone was too thick to hear anything substantial over my own panicked breathing.

Fuck, fuck, fuck!

I'd been so close!

But I wasn't alone. The wall closing had produced a T in the road, and my head swiveled to meet the eyes of a pair of surprised feminine Runners, looking just as lost as I felt.

I cursed under my breath and decided to go right down the long hallway, away from the two. The last thing I needed was to get into a fight with no weapon in hand. It was the best I could do, taking the next left to try and circle the box that held the single most important person in my life.

I'd just have to hope that when I found my way in, I wouldn't be too late.

Hang on, cowboy. I'm coming.

Cam

What if she's telling the truth?

With Aubrey safely out of the way, I turned my attention back to Ella.

The walls closed around us to form a box, the opening that'd been created closin' as quickly as it'd been made. No way out, and with a girl crazier than a bed bug with a knife at my back, I knew I only had one chance at this.

One chance to win. One chance to make it out alive.

One chance to make the Church proud. To make me proud. If I succeed in this I'd finally prove im not a failure. That I can live up to my family name.

I turned, lungin' for the knife in Ella's hand. She lashed out with the blade, laying a heavy slash to my forearm that was absolutely going to fuck up one of my favorite tattoos.

Fucking cunt.

But a little scratch wasn't gonna deter me. I caught her arm, stalling another pass and more damage, strikin' her wrist against the stone wall. The knife clattered to the floor as she gasped, her look of determination cracking into fear as my booted foot went over the weapon, dragging it closer to me.

Ella shook off my grip, divin' for the weapon, but I was too fast, bending to pick it up fluidly, the tip of the weapon instantly pressed to her jugular as I crowded her back against the wall.

She thought she was going up against a rookie.

As if I hadn't spent my entire fuckin' life preparing for this. As if my family wasn't known as big player killers every time they stepped foot onto the island.

Her breaths came in panicky pants, desperate tears forming in her eyes.

A test, my mind warned. She looked pitiful. She looked scared.

It looked real enough to make my heart twist.

But I knew better now. I knew I had to end this.

"P-please! I wasn't going to actually kill you! You've gotta know that! Cam, I trust you. You trust me. We're a team!"

"Is that right?" I teased, the events of the last few hours rolling through my mind like tumbleweeds in the desert. The picture painting itself in waves of fury, like a late summer sunset—blood red. "Because the way I see it, you've been getting fat as a tick on my hard work, waiting for a moment to get rid of me so you could get to the end. Let me believe you were loyal so I'd help your worthless ass."

"C-Cam, no!" she begged, her voice cracking on a sob. "Please, please! You don't understand!"

Like hell I don't understand. This place is my whole fuckin' life!

"Please spare me the fuckin' waterworks, darlin'. You signed up. You chose to be here just like I did. I don't care what your reason—"

"I didn't sign up!" Ella shouted, fat tears rolling down her splotchy, red face. "I didn't choose this! Why would anyone choose this hell?"

Is she joking?

Devil's Playground got away with many things. Murder being the biggest. And all because people gave their consent. They *signed* up for their own murder *and* for it to be televised. All for the chance of winning big at the end.

I reared back with a laugh. "Ella, ain't no use in lyin' to me. Of course you signed up. I reckon you're regrettin' it now that it's gotten ugly. But you signed on the dotted line like everyone else."

"Cam, I swear, I didn't. I never wanted to be here. I fucked up, but I wouldn't ever choose to be here."

Now, wasn't that a likely story? Preying on my sensibility, my natural lenience.

I almost felt proud, and I knew Ma would love it. She always did favor social strategy over just plain killin'.

But it was a bunch of poppycock. It was a core element of the Games, the most basic rule. We all made the call to be here. Signed up with your own pen to the paper. Read the contracts. Knew what we were gettin' into. Fame, fortune, and death. Whatever the outcome—it was our choice.

It was *always* the player's choice.

"C'mon, you gotta be able to come up with a better lie than that, Ella. This is just really fuckin' sad."

"I'm not lying!" she insisted, her dark eyes meeting mine angrily. "Why the fuck would I sign up to be hunted like an animal?"

"Well, technically, you didn't," I corrected in a drawl. "That'd be Hide N' Seek. You signed up to run a maze. Just so happens—"

"I didn't sign up!" she screamed, her tears dripping from her chin.

I pressed the tip of the blade against her jugular.

It'd be so fuckin' easy to kill her right now. Take her life for makin' a fool outta me.

Make a show of it, Pa crooned lovingly in my ear.

But I wasn't no PKer. I wouldn't do it. And there was just something about the way she mentioned fucking up that had me pausing.

It's a test, my mind reminded me. But even so, it would be a disservice for me to not at least try and see how far this *test* would go.

"Alright, yeah, let's pretend I believe you. If you didn't sign up, how is it that you managed to get through the door? You had to sign the contracts. Go through the physical. The prep tent."

Her eyes narrowed at me.

"I'm a felon," she spat. "My options were to either rot in prison or try and change my circumstances."

Prison? For some reason, Ella didn't seem like much of a criminal to me. Sure, she might have been trying to plot my murder the entire time, but that was inside the game. Outside the walls of Devil's Playground?

I couldn't quite make heads or tails of it.

"That doesn't make any fucking sense, Ella," I admitted.

"I got caught, okay? B and E, not supposed to be a big deal, skateboarding with my friends, but the school they were building wasn't done on the second level and we didn't know that security guard was there and—"

"What did they charge you with?"

I didn't want to waste precious time. Each moment I stood there with Ella was another moment keeping me away from the finish line.

And another minute separated from Aubrey.

"Manslaughter."

Okay, maybe that made more sense.

"Fitting," I said bitterly. "Given you're a PKer too."

"Not yet," she said breathlessly, her eyes darting from mine to the knife pressed against her throat. "But I'll do whatever I fucking have to to get out of here."

"You're unbelievable," I muttered.

"And you're no better," she spat out, her voice raising with a twinge of desperation added to it. "What's the difference between dying here at your hands or in a fucking cell? At least down here I had a chance to try and earn my freedom."

"Stop lying!" I shouted, pullin' the knife back a little so I could slam her into the wall, knocking the air clear out of her lungs.

I am better! Even if the darkness wanted me to end it all, I wouldn't be like them.

Ella spluttered and coughed, nearly doubling over if it wasn't for the threat of the blade keeping her upright. "I'm not lying!" she said yet again. "This shit is fucked up. I don't want to hurt anyone. I didn't even want to hurt you!"

Pain like a migraine was starting to make the vision in my left eye spotty, Pa's voice in my head getting louder—more insistent.

Kill her, go on. Make a show of it, Camilla, he sneered, that pulsing pressure making it hard to focus.

It would be so easy. So fuckin' easy.

As quick as snapping her neck. I wouldn't even need to use the knife. She says she was in prison for manslaughter, but her body didn't show any of the hardness someone in prison should have. It would take mere seconds, and her life would be slippin' from her cold, dead fingers.

But that wouldn't be making a show of it. Naw, she needed to suffer.

Ella'd betrayed me after all. She was going to hurt me. Probably would hurt Aubrey as well. Even after all the time it took me to help her through the maze... none of it mattered.

Not to her.

Not to me.

Betrayal meant *punishment.* It meant getting even. It meant showing the world that I wasn't one to play with. But a tiny, oddly muffled voice whispered, *What if she's tellin' the truth?*

I reckoned that if Ella hadn't signed up to play the Devil's Playground willingly... that changed everything. It was one thing if we were all on the same playing field, so to speak, chosen for ourselves to be here knowing the risk that we'd never walk back out.

If Ella was telling the truth and she'd been forced to sign up... Only the good Lord was able to judge her for what she did in order to survive. Now, that didn't exempt her from *consequences.* She'd still tried to make a fool out of me. Threatened Aubrey.

Naw, now that was something I couldn't just forgive... or forget.

That deserved a bit of penance.

"Alright," I said slowly, watching relief flood her features. "I won't kill you."

Feeble, half-trembling words of gratitude spilled from her lips between sobs as I pulled the knife away. The girl relaxed, a big mistake on her part. It left her open to my attack.

Without warning, I kicked her leg out toward me, making her catch her balance with it outstretched. I reared back, stomping down on her shin with all the strength I had, snapping the frail bones with a sickening crunch.

Ella screamed, falling to the ground, clutching her destroyed leg.

I brought my tracker close to my face, ready to scroll through the comments and take suggestions on how I should punish her. But I was met with something I'd never seen before.

In the top corner, where my view count should have been... there was a big red *zero*.

What the actual—

I didn't know it was possible for me to get angrier until that moment. Heat rushed over me, flushing my face and entire body. It had my head spinning and my muscles seizing.

They shut my stream off. This wasn't the first time it happened in Devil's Playground. They did it whenever it suited them.

But it was the first time it ever happened to a Weston.

Not only had she tried to kill me, but because of her, my views were zero! The whole world would miss out on what it meant to punish those who'd wronged me. I would never get my redemption.

Maybe you should kill her because of that, a voice whispered. *An even better punishment.*

But the other nagging voice was back. The one that told me the Architects wouldn't have shut off my views if they wanted the world to see what was happening.

They didn't want them to know.

I pushed all those thoughts to the back, not willing to go down the rabbit hole they threatened to take me.

Regardless, she still needs to learn her lesson.

I leaned down close to her face, my lip curled in anger. "Now we're even, darlin'. Play hard. Win, win."

Aubrey

How about you make me, cowboy?

I was close. I knew it. I'd followed the hallway to the right, fingers dragging against the stone searching for any indents or crevices in the wall, then looped inward.

The problem was, the greyish concrete slabs all looked the same. *Felt* the same when I frantically ran my hands against them while searching.

It would've been enough to drive me insane if I wasn't so homed in on saving Cam. I could feel their presence, close but just out of reach. It might've been the insanity that'd slowly gnawed at my consciousness since I got into the maze, but I swore it was really *them*.

They're right in the middle, I know it.

Like the moth to the flame I was drawn to them, a compulsion that was only getting stronger and stronger. Making me desperate, crazy unlike anything I'd ever experienced. Anxiety tightening my throat as I searched for my way in.

Distantly, I could hear others in the maze. The traps going off as they tried to get to the end. The Screaming. Panicking. Scrambling.

But not me. I was focused.

The other runners meant nothing to me. They could burn and crush themselves to death until there was nothing but silence and my blood rushing in my ears. I wanted the one who ignited these new feelings in me, who made my heart race and stomach flutter with need.

I couldn't let anything else distract me.

I *wouldn't*.

Cam's presence was calling to me like a beacon, reaching through the walls and guiding me closer and closer. I could taste them on the tip of my tongue, the sunlight and warm haylike flavour of a person who'd spent a lifetime outside. Feel the warmth of their skin against mine. My body vibrated with the anticipation of seeing them again, the siren call of their steady calm pulling me closer, closer—

Until I hit a dead end right on the other side of where Cam should be.

Fuck.

They're so close. I know they're just behind this wall.

But just because it was a dead end, it didn't mean it was deserted.

A familiar man was there, inspecting the wall I needed to break through.

A man worth a million dollars.

The one that killed *her*. The one that decided to attach himself to the group that attempted to end me. *And Cam.*

Hiram Wolff.

When he turned around and saw me, his eyes widened in a mix of fear and surprise.

Good, he stil had some sense then.

He raised his filthy hands, which were now empty, to help shield his unmasked face. Worse for wear didn't even begin to cover it. The man looked positively like he was on his last legs. Same vibes as a raccoon with mange, barely holding on.

But where is the leader? The guy Cam called Elijah? Maybe they had a falling out.

"Look, I'm not trying to—" Hiram started as I began to move towards him.

As if I gave a fuck about this washed up shell of a man while my partner was in there with that two-faced cunt.

I marched past him, shoving him out of the way to look at the wall. His body slammed into the side of the maze, a pained grunt escaping from him as I ran my hands on the smooth surface.

No indent like Ella found. How the fuck am I supposed to get inside?

"Ow, what the fuck—"

"Shut. Up."

The venom in my voice must have been enough to let him know I wasn't messing around. How was I supposed to concentrate with him yapping in my ear?

I only wished it would've just been Hiram who decided to bother me, kicking myself for not taking the threat that Elijah was near by more seriously.

"Hey, look who it is."

Are you fucking kidding me?

Elijah decided to show his face. If I'd had more time, I would've gotten revenge on him for Cam. But saving them was more important than killing him.

For now.

"I don't have time for your half-witted fuckery, limp dick," I shot back, not even looking at him.

The looming silence was broken by Elijah's sputtering laughter.

I ignored him, continuously searching for some type of trap that would open the wall. My conviction, even with the overwhelming evidence that I may in fact be mistaken, was fuelled in part by desperation. I knew that ever second that ticked by was another that Ella could've—I pushed the idea away, rejecting it entirely.

Cam was going to be fine. I was going to get to them.

There has to be a way in.

Just thinking about them behind the walls with that rat was driving me insane. Ella was going to kill them, or at least try. And with Cam's backwoods, "Let's all hold hands and not PK" mind-set, I wasn't sure how far they'd go to protect themselves.

The near-constant chanting inside my head threatened to drive me right over the edge.

Cam.

Kill the bitch.

Cam.

Find the trap.

Cam.

Slice her throat.

Cam. Cam. Cam. Cam—

Rough hands grabbed my shoulders and pulled me back. I let out a feral scream, swinging my arms at the person.

And clocked the man right in his weak-ass jaw.

I wasn't surprised that I was met with Elijah's now-unmasked face—or that he'd had the audacity to touch me. What was shocking was that between the last time I'd culled his little team of henchman and now that he'd managed to pick up two more masked lackeys. They jumped into action, lunging at me with masks glowing in matching neon yellow as soon as my fist made contact with his face.

"Let me go, you shit for brains!"

I headbutted one of them. The pain of it numbed by the pure satisfaction of the audible *crunch* and seeing blood profusely pouring out from under the lip of the mask.

"Really thought you could get the upper hand? *Ha!* Pussy boys don't fucking scare me."

I grabbed the other by his arm that was still holding onto me and pulled him closer until I could sink my teeth into the flesh.

His scream echoed throughout the hallway as I punctured his skin, spitting a chunk of him out onto the floor with the sickly, coppery taste of his blood coating my tongue.

Another scream rang out, but it wasn't any of the men surrounding me.

It was a *girl*.

It came again, my head whipping around to find the source. Not that'd do me any good. I was trapped in a dead end with four men and no where to go but back through.

It wasn't until the third scream that I realized it was coming from behind the wall.

Is that Cam?

Too high, right? Couldn't be.

Still, my stomach squirmed uncomfortably.

I didn't really believe in God, but I prayed to whichever fucked-up one Cam believed in, hoping it would somehow give them the strength to slit that bitch's throat.

I turned to the boys, a sigh falling from my lips.

I guess I need to deal with them before I open the wall.

What an inconvenience.

I ran at them with a guttural yell. The one on the right panicked, stumbling multiple steps backward, allowing me to tackle the other to the ground.

I got a few good punched to his head in before the other tried to come at me, seeming to remember he was infact supposed to be apart of this fight. I grabbed onto one of his punches and used his momentum to force him to the ground, only narrowly dodging Elijah's ham-like fist coming at my cheek. The boy who'd been thrown to the floor using my distraction at the near-miss to grab my hair and *pull*.

"Cheap move, you cunt!" I screamed and maneuvered myself so my booted foot could kick him right in the balls.

As far as I was concerned, the only person who was allowed to touch my hair was Cam.

It was just enough to create an opening for me to scramble through, earning me some precious space between me and the group of attacking men.

I narrowed my eyes at Elijah, who returned it with an annoyed look.

"Letting them do your dirty work for you, huh? No wonder Cam thinks you're a no good pussy with no chance in Hell at winning this thing."

His jaw ticked, and in a blink, he was rushing at me. Movements lacking control of finesse in his anger.

Now we're getting somewhere.

Pussy boy has a fucking ego, shocker.

He was strong—and fast—but I was faster. My small frame helped me dodge punch after punch, and when I saw my opening, I used my foot to push him back toward the group in a vicious kick to his gut.

Hiram was still there, panic lacing his features, letting the rest of his rag-tag group of fucking losers fight on his behalf.

Disgusting coward. No wonder Vic wants you dead.

I brushed the sweat from my brow, cocking my head at Elijah and his lackeys. It was obvious none of them really *wanted* to fight, since their eyes kept darting to Elijah and then back to me, waiting for some type of order.

"You need a break, limp dick?"

"Stop calling me that!" Elijah snarled, anger twisting his face.

The pinging of my watch told me the audience didn't want me to stop–or at least I hoped that's what the messages said. Who the fuck had time to check in a moment like this?

The screaming coming from inside the wall continued for a long while, and every now and then I would make out something that sounded like a moan, but the fuckers kept me just busy enough that I hadn't had time to listen fully.

What I *had* noticed, though, were the small circular cracks on the walls around us. They were evenly spaced and just about throat-length.

But where is the damn trigger?

"You wouldn't be getting so mad if it wasn't true," I pushed with a small laugh.

Elijah's neck and ears turned red, his freckles threatening to disappear under a heavy blush. He lifted his arms, knife in hand and ready to charge... Until the rumbling started again.

The maze is resetting again. How?

I looked around wildly, trying to make sure that I wasn't one of the unlucky ones who were about to be crushed. But there was only one wall moving.

The one behind me.

My heart lodged in my throat. Hope filling my chest.

Cam.

And, lo and behold, there they were, waiting as the wall slowly descended into the floor. Shoulders moving with their panting breaths and still damp, but not a scratch on them.

Thank you, God!

I started toward them, ready to shove my fist down the rat's throat, but... Cam was *alone*.

Where the fuck is she?

Her crumpled body didn't come into view until the wall was fully down.

She was on the floor, holding her leg, tears running down her face. The leg in question bent at an odd angle with bone peircing her pale flesh.

Their eyes were trained on the rat. The ghost of a smile was on their lips, telling me that they liked to see her brought down a peg as much as I did.

Did they break her fucking leg?

It was in that moment, when the headhunters were screaming for my death and the rat was crying for mercy, that I truly fell in love with Cam. Time standing still for several long beats as she turns and our eyes met, smile growing and becoming relieved.

"Hey, Peaches."

They're just as fucked up as I am.

Calm and collected, even as chaos reigned around us. The darkness that'd been hiding inside them was finally out for all to see. And it just happened to match mine perfectly.

Fuck, I'm so in love. They're perfect. Absolutely perfect.

I couldn't help the girlish giggle that fell from my lips. I looked back at the boys with a wide smile. Seeing Cam safe must've done something to clear my mind because as soon as I turned, I saw the small indent on the floor that would undoubtedly set off the trap.

I ran to it, dodging Elijah's attempt to grab me until I got to the place where the wall met the floor, sliding across the dirty ground like a soccer star to smash the trigger.

The only warning was our watches turning red before the spikes shot out across the hallway, embedding themselves into the boys' heads and necks. Their blood splattered everywhere, painting my pink outfit with streaks of crimson.

Turns out the rat was right about something. It adds a good pop of color to an otherwise monochromatic look, especially since it wasnt mine.

Except for one. Hiram had already been half cowering against the wall. It was hard to believe this loser had ever been a winner in the Games, but I'd guessed it didn't take a lot of bravery to play Hide n' Seek, but it wasn't enough to save him. A spike impaling him through the chest and shoulder.

Elijah had dropped to the ground when the trap was triggered, his eyes widened and fearful. Now, he pushed himself up and ran back down the hallway, leaving his knife behind.

Lucky cunt.

I dashed to gather it, looking back at Cam with a wicked smile that was returned in spades.

"That's my girl," they praised, lighting my skin with excited feelings.

They don't even know what's coming.

I threw the knife directly at Ella, embedding it between her eyes. She didn't even have time to react, her body falling slack against the cold cement floor. Wide eyes open, forever in a state of pained shock.

Her death is even more satisfying than Natalie's could ever be.

"Fucking finally," I said with a giggle. "She fucking deserved it, that cun—"

Cam let out a heavy sigh, their toned shoulders sagging with disappointment as the familiar buzz of our watches warned everyone of my PK.

"Can you stop killing people already? I had it under control."

My smile widened.

"How about you make me, cowboy?"

Their nostrils flared.

"*Don't*, Aubrey," they warned, the growl in their tone like a lick between my legs.

I readied myself, turning ever so slightly down the hall. High on adrenaline and the image of Cam's cruelty. I wanted them to show me what else they'd been keeping from me. How far they'd go.

And I know exactly how to push them right over that line.

I didn't respond. Instead, I shot them a coy wink, paired with a twitch of my fingers in a little wave, and darted down the hallway.

CAM

HAVE YOU LEARNED YOUR LESSON?

Aubrey's golden hair whipped around the corner, and I saw red.

It was beyond temptation.

It was fuckin' cheek.

My little bloodied angel damn near flew down the hall as I chased after her. Her panicked breathing and the sound of her boots against the concrete far too loud if she was actually tryin' to escape me.

We should've been going after Elijah and Hiram, but it would have to wait.

There wasn't no fuckin' way I was lettin' her get away with it. Not this time. Not with the weight of everything that'd happened pressin' down on me like bricks.

How quickly I'd lost control of this game even after a lifetime of training was stifling as late August humidity. Hard to breathe around, sticky.

Totally un-fuckin'-missable.

Lord have mercy, I was tired of bein' tested. If I was judge n' jury, it was time for a bit of reward.

And in Aubrey's case, a whole hell of a lot of punishment.

I hadn't been part of my plan to end up on a team I'd spent

the game carrying. Even less so gettin' emotionally involved with another fuckin' Runner in the confines of the maze.

Losing all my viewership because some loudmouth reckoned that her life was worth more to me than winnin' this game. Not that'd even made a difference now, not since Aubrey'd snuffed her clean out.

Fuckin' menace of a woman.

Once I catch her, she'll be sorry.

This place, the Architects that ran it—hell, even my own *family*—wanted me to be a monster. And I was sick of denying them the satisfaction.

Besides, as much as I wanted to ignore it, there was a part of me that'd loved watchin' Ella beg. The power of it. Her dirty, tear-streaked face as she stared up at me, hopin'—nah, *prayin'*— that I'd roll over and accept her bullshit excuses for turnin' on me.

Better than a cold beer after mowin' the lawn.

Even if, in the back of my mind, doubt was still naggin' at me that she might've been forced into the maze. Was it really possible? Were there players who'd found their way inside the game without their consent?

Had to be, didn't it? Why else punish me by cutting off my feed? Even now my watch was lifeless on my wrist, absent of the constant stream of notifications I'd quickly gotten used to thanks to my viewers' comments.

Watchers made up a decent portion of this game, offering up helpful hints of what direction to go in and how to get to the end quicker. Without them? Things would be a whole lot more difficult.

Still, the break from my family was... relievin'.

Regardless of whether she'd been tellin' stories, the truth, or something in between, I did want to make Ella suffer for breakin' my trust.

And damn, did I ever make a show of it. The broken leg was just the beginning. There was *so* much I wanted to do.

But then my little angel came around and plucked it right from my hands.

It was... too much.

Embarrassin'. Naw, not just embarrassin', humiliatin'.

I needed to take back control.

And there she was, purposefully goading me into takin' my bad mood out on her. Getting incredibly close to uncappin' the black, tar-like substance that'd been pressin' against the lids of my insides since I'd stepped foot inside this arena.

Not the valuable Texas crude that I'd stumbled upon once in shooting practice. Naw, this was something much more volatile. Violent. Just beggin' to be let out so it could wreak havoc on everything.

And she wanted all of it. The excitement on her face when she'd seen what I had done to Ella was undeniable. She'd been waiting for her chance to kill the girl and the moment she saw it, she pounced. A cougar and a fuckin' fawn.

It only made me angrier. She took my chance from me. I had the chance to make a show of it. Had a chance to finally show Pa what I had up my sleeve.

She ruined it in an instant like it was nothin' and wanted to use my anger for her own entertainment. But she had no idea what she was askin' for.

I let it run wild as I gave chase, my booted feet poundin' hard against the concrete as I followed Aubrey's panting breaths. We had to be close to the end of the maze by now—even with the changes, it couldn't be far off.

Not that I had a hope in capitalistic Hell to rank now.

Fuck.

But in it's place she offered me somethin' much better.

My skin was hot, sweat beginnin' to bead along my forehead and neck with the effort of keepin' pace. My lungs were burnin' with the need for air. My muscles itching as adrenaline rushed through my veins.

Aubrey's back came into view, forcing me to go faster, a roar of anger escaping me. Her head turned just enough to the side to catch a glimpse of me behind her, blonde hair streaked in coppery crimson whipping behind her with each step.

And there's that fuckin' smile again.

"When I catch you, Peaches, you'll wish you never met me," I hollered down the corridor. "You may never walk straight again."

I was close enough that I could hear the way my promise made her breath catch. Could practically smell the blonde's arousal as my fingers slid through the ends of her hair, just far enough ahead that I couldn't quite get purchase. Like she could sense the close call, she picked up the pace, skiddin' so hard that, as she took the next corner, her hand hit the ground to stabilize her.

I'd hunted enough rabbits in my time to see the signs of a healthy animal fightin' for its life. And that's the vibe Aubrey gave, her strong legs taking her further and further down the hallway, eclipsin' even my longer stride.

Unfortunately for her, I was more motivated.

And resourceful.

How many times did she think I'd allow her bad fuckin' attitude to go unchecked? How many times was I gonna let her disobey me with a smile on her face?

These weren't little things.

I didn't ask her to do the dishes or hang the laundry.

It was disobedience through and through. And she *knew* what would happen if she continued to disobey me. That made it all the more treacherous.

I'd told her not to kill Ella—my friend, even if she'd been a lyin', traitorous bitch—and she'd chosen to do it anyway. But I didn't know what made me angrier. That she was my friend and had been schemin' against me, or that my ability to actually prove myself to the family was stolen from me.

Call it insanity brought on by grief, call it fallin' into darkness. Whatever it was, I knew that there was only one thing awaitin' her once I caught her.

Somethin' so sinfully sweet. Somethin' that had been lurking in the back of my mind since I first laid eyes on her.

Since I first tasted the delicious nectar between her thighs.

Punishment.

And this time, I wasn't gonna go easy on her. I'd firmly shut out my conscience, and there was nothing left but the darkness whisperin' dirty things to me. Depraved things.

It was high time that someone taught Aubrey a few hard lessons.

Patience. Humility. Some good old-fashioned southern manners.

And I reckoned I was gonna be the one to do it.

I unlooped the rope hangin' from my belt, fashioning it quickly into a lasso. As excitin' as the chase was, it really was more better for the prey. For the predator? All the enjoyment came after I'd wrapped my teeth around her jugular.

She turned another corner, but this time she peeked back at me. There was just a millisecond where her face fully came into view before disappearin' again, but I still saw every last detail.

The low, warm light in her beautiful blue eyes.

The sweat shinin' on her face in a delicious sheen.

And the twisted smile that told me she was just yearnin' for the moment where I finally got my fingers locked around her neck.

I gripped the corner, usin' it to propel me faster. The clompin' of my boots echoed through the deserted hallways.

If there were other players around, they stayed away. *Good.*

If anyone even dared get between the two of us, I wouldn't hesitate to cut them down. PKer be damned.

I wasn't the same Cam that entered the maze. The little temptation changed me.

For better or worse, we were about to find out.

She was fuckin' fast. But all I needed was just one little slip up.

And it came on the third sharp turn she tried to make.

Aubrey stumbled, and I took the opportunity to make my

throw, the rope closin' around her neck. I pulled hard, chokin' her clean off her feet and to the floor. But that didn't deter her, the gasp of pain and surprise preceding the sound of her tryin' to scrabble away along the stone, perfect pink nails caked with blood and grime.

A wild animal caught in the trap.

I held the rope taut, bearin' down on her like a nightmare. A fox waitin' just outside the chicken coop.

If Aubrey wanted to flirt with the wickedness in me, who was I to deny her the privilege? I'd let my demons loose. Worship her like the Virgin, perverted into my personal whore of darkness. A saint brought to life for the sheer purpose of quakin' around my fingers and tongue.

"Cam," she choked, gripping at the rope. "You're... You're hurting me."

"Good," I snarled, falling to my knees to grab her ankle, pulling her across the floor and onto my lap. She fought hard, kicking and screamin' as I undid the belt around her waist, yanking down that foolishly small skirt and the little spandex shorts attached to it to bare her round, pale ass to me. I smirked at the wet spot I found.

She must be sorely missing her panties.

"Somebody needs to teach you how to fuckin' behave," I snarled. "When I give you a direct order, I expect it to be followed."

A clawed hand came close to my face, and I caught it, using the length of the rope to bind her wrists behind her back before attaching it to her ankles, turning it into a quick and effective hogtie.

I yanked the rope taut with a grunt of frustration, leaving myself just enough space to have access to her ass.

"Awful sick of this attitude, Peaches," I muttered.

"Fuck. You," she spat out, her furious eyes meetin' mine. "Let me go, Cam."

I struck, the clap of my palm against her ass cheek ricocheting from the cement walls.

Aubrey shouted and cursed. I used my free hand to tug the rope again, the knot tightening until she was forced to scrunch up, baring her ass to me some more.

"Enough."

Her breath left her in a trembling gasp, real fear in her blue eyes as they met mine. It had a powerful shiver running through my body.

I wanted to see more of her like this. And they may have cut off my views, but hers were still alive and well.

I paused to look through her tracker, reading the messages aloud.

"Needy whore mewling like a cat, one comments," I said with a dark chuckle. She squirmed underneath me. "Spread her wider. Where's the bat? They're loving you, peaches."

She made a pathetic sound that had my pussy clentching.

"Why don't we give them what they want?"

"*Cam—*"

"Count." It was an order. *A demand.* No room left for negotiation.

She sniffled. Almost like she was truly scared. "C-cam, don't. Please..."

"Until you start counting," I said with a vicious strike against her ass that made her scream. She screamed so prettily. I wanted to record it just so I could play it over and over again. Maybe I'd force her to watch it when we got out while I fucked her. "These are just for fun."

"Please!" Another. "I'm sorry!" Another. "Cam!" Again and again with her pleading until I heard the first, trembled number. "One."

More. More. More.

The darkness was chanting, consuming my entire being. Her screams and begging only made me lose myself in it that much more.

But this time I wasn't sure I wanted to resurface.

"Good girl," I praised softly, my hand stinging from the impact. "I think twenty-five is fair, given the amount of sass I've endured tonight."

Tears pricked at the corners of her eyes, her face turning down toward the floor. A degrading position that only a disobedient whore deserved.

She'll redeem herself soon.

"This is so fucking humiliating," she whispered, hands fisting on the ground.

I smirked, clapping down on her ass again to a sulkily muttered, "Two."

"That's the point, darlin'. How do you think I feel when you openly disobey me?"

Again and again I struck her, until her ass was rosy with the evidence of my anger. *Such a beautiful color.*

My fingers stung, palm and fingers swollen with my efforts, and yet Aubrey's cries weren't enough. Her desperation was barely beginning to scratch the itch my demon commanded.

If I had the whole night, I'd punish her before worshiping her delicious cunt like no one had before. I wanted her all alone. *All mine.* Wanted to tie her to the bed and have my wicked way with her until she was so wanton she wouldn't know her own name.

"Adjust," I ordered, forcing Aubrey onto her knees awkwardly where she was still bent across my lap. The change of angle bore her pussy to me. If I wanted to, I could fuck her lying, useless cunt while she ached from her punishment. But not yet.

Tenderly, I rubbed her sore ass, a moment of reprieve amidst the vicious torment. Every pathetic little moan and whine falling from her lips was better than the Devil's fiddle itself, and Jesus, was I ever in the mood to play. My fingers grazed dangerously lower, preparing to strike against her rosy lower lips when I realized that she was damp, her aching slit leaking through her folds to leave sweet, sticky nectar along her thighs and dampening my pants.

The traitorous slut was enjoying her punishment. I slapped her cunt hard, making her keen loudly, her panting breaths taking on a new intensity.

"Nineteen," she whispered, half sobbing. "Please, Cam, I'll be good. Just... Please..."

We both knew it was a lie. No matter how much I punished her, there would be no changing who she truly was.

But that made it fun for both of us.

"Spread yourself," I whispered, leaning down close to her ear. My lips brushed the reddened tip. "Awfully hard to be wet and sorry at the same time, Peaches."

"C-cam, p-please... I—"

"You're a nasty little whore is what you are. Spread. Yourself."

She wobbled a little, twisting her hands to obey me until I had a clear view of the pearl of nerves that lived at the apex of her thighs. Briefly, I considered touching her with kindness, giving her the relief that a release would provide after enduring well over half of her punishment.

But how was my dog meant to learn to behave if I didn't maintain a firm hand when it came to discipline?

Fuck me, did I hate getting bit.

My first strike made her scream, her eyes squeezing shut in a mix of bliss and agony, the muscles of her tight hole contracting in anticipation.

"Twenty," came Aubrey's trembling whisper on the tail end of a sob, the other numbers tumbling from her lips as I continued my assault. "Twenty-one, twenty-two, twenty-three, twenty-four..."

I paused, cradling her shaking body in one arm as she sobbed, fat tears pooling on the concrete below her head.

"Have you learned your lesson?"

"Yes, Cam—"

"Cam?" I sneered, disgust welling up inside me. "Is that how a dog sees their owner? As a friend whose first name they can use? So fuckin' pedestrian that they can call them any old thing?"

"N-no, I mean..." she said quickly, licking her dry lips. "Master." It was barely a whisper. I wouldn't have heard it if she'd so much as shifted her weight. "Sir?" Aubrey's eyes met mine, the question in them. I nodded. "Sir, please."

I stroked my fingers through her soaked center, a single one dipping inside to begin the slow stretch of her cunt. Aubrey reacted immediately, a soft whimper escaping her lips.

"You were a good girl. Counted well..." I reasoned, inserting a second finger to scissor them inside her, twisting my hand to arc my fingers into the place that made her legs quiver. "Suppose I could make you come."

"Please!" she gasped, pressing her throbbing opening backwards into my hand. "More, Cam—"

I chuckled, my free hand cracking down on her sore ass, making her jolt. "Naw, Peaches, you don't tell me what to do." I added a third finger, smirking at the stretch as I fucked them into her quickly, my thumb finding her clit, rubbing it in tight little circles. "If I want to give you more, I will. If I want you to lie there trembling in a pool of your own tears, I'll do that instead."

She started to speak, but I continued over her, my voice rising slightly.

"Only thing I want to hear past those pretty pink lips of yours is you singing my praises, Aubrey," I said, fingers twisting.

I should've been embarrassed, being out in the open like this, but it diddn't matter anymore, I didn't have any reason to hold back. There was no test. No bigger task sent from God to prove my faith. If anything, God sent her to me to enjoy. This woman was *mine*. And I'd use her, ride her, and put her back as wet as I saw fit.

She gasped, a soft shudder moving through her little frame as I arched closer and closer to her sweet spot. Her hands flexed in their restraints as her back bowed feebly.

"Cam—yes! Please!"

Putty in my hands, that was how she felt as I continued to plunge my fingers in and out of her, Aubrey's sweet, heady arousal dripping from her abused entrance and down my wrist in thin lines. She didn't just like to be dominated. Naw, Aubrey liked to be *humiliated*.

I realized it from the first moment I had her against the maze wall. I watched her as she looked through the comments, her breathing getting harder and harder.

She wanted them to see. Wanted them to participate.

And who am I to deny her the pleasure? I was taught to make a show of it, and I would take that to heart. I would take every moment I could to show the world what a good little *whore* my little angel was.

"You like knowing people could be watching, don't you?" I hissed at her, renewing my efforts. "Like knowin' all those faceless creeps are watching me touch your sweet little pussy."

She bit down hard on her lip, a pathetic attempt at keeping her loud, desperate whines quiet as they tumbled from her lips. A new sound for each sensation as I fucked her useless cunt with my fingers. Using the ropes, I sat her up on her knees, forcing her heavily down on my hand.

"You know what good little cowgirls do for their masters, Peaches?" I asked against her neck, kissing the warm, gold skin before dragging my teeth upward to nip at her ear.

"N-no," she whispered, panting and wriggling, her hips moving slightly to chase my hand.

"They *ride*."

It was as much an order as an answer, leaving no room for argument.

Aubrey's hips jerked into motion. She was either too worked up or too tired to argue with my command as she bounced up and down on my hand, pleasuring herself with a string of hissed curses and praises.

I'd like to force her to lick my cunt, to have her make a mess of that beautiful face of hers while tasting exactly what all those little noises and obedience did for me, but there wasn't time.

Never seemed to be enough time in this fuckin' place.

Aubrey's tits bounced as she rode me. I pushed her crop top up, freeing them. They were so perfectly kissable looking, especially as they jerked with everymovement. My imagination took me to a place where I'd use a strap on to fuck her entirely too brave mouth until she choked, then watched as the soft curves of her body moved as I drove her into the mattress of some fancy-ass hotel.

An idea for once we'd won this thing.

In the meantime, I pressed my fingers hard against my girl's sweet spot, dragging her backwards until she hit the stones hard, her cunt bared to me as I bent to meet my hand, lips wrapping around her clit for a firm suck that had her screaming.

"I'm going to come! Fuck! Cam, please!" Aubrey gasped and moaned, feebly pressing against my mouth.

But I didn't need no direction to help me make my woman come as I circled my tongue over the bud of nerves. It wasn't long before Aubrey's moans hit their peak, dissolving into half-sobs of pleasure as her muscles clenched hard around my fingers for my effort.

Tears slipped from the corners of Aubrey's eyes, her breaths heavy as she rejoined me from space.

"Untie me," she whispered, her eyes finding mine as I wiped my mouth. "I really need to kiss you."

I smiled, leaning forward to oblige.

"Good girl."

The bodies were right where we left them, hanging from the spikes, their blood dripping into a puddle on the floor.

I almost felt sorry for the two new people Elijah recruited.

The Church taught him well.

He used people until he couldn't anymore and tried his best

to keep his hands from getting dirty unless absolutely necessary. But at the end of the day, they knew what they'd signed up for and had the chance to leave before it came to this.

But the one who held my attention was the Architect. Hiram got caught up in the crossfire, no doubt a pawn Elijah was going to use to win my parents over.

And while I might not be able to use Hiram, it made me happy to know Elijah wouldn't either.

"I think it was somewhere over here," Aubrey muttered as she searched the ground.

Something caught my eye. The slight movement of light reflected off the blood pouring from the wound in his neck. The slight rise and fall of his chest.

And the *wheezing*.

"Hold on," I said and ducked between the spikes that held the bodies up. I got closer and bent down so I could look him in the eyes.

They were open and staring right at me.

Excitement zapped through my body.

Seeing that Aubrey had set off the trap, I assumed the kill had been attributed to her, but if his heart was still beating…

"Show me where it is."

"Here!" I followed Aubrey's pointed finger as she beamed at me.

"Good girl," I praised, giving her a smile. "You don't know how much you've done for me."

Not so much a sin sent to tempt me, but maybe an angel sent to put me on the right path.

"The Architect is still alive," I said, weaving through the spikes and coming to a halt where the trap was located.

"The spikes are probably the only thing keeping him from bleeding out," she mused, casting a glance back at him. "Pity, the money would have been nice."

"You don't care about that," I pointed out.

"I don't," she admitted with a wicked smile that had my heart skipping a beat. *Bloodthirsty indeed.*

"I'll share it with you when we win this thing," I promised and pushed the indent that activated the trap.

The bodies fell to the floor with a thump.

A sound came out of the Architect's throat. I turned to him, slowly closing the space between us. His fingers were twitching, but nothing else was moving. Not even his eyes, which were forced into a wide, never-ending stare as his life force bled out of him.

When I got close enough, I placed my booted foot on his throat and leaned forward just enough to put pressure on his windpipe.

His death was a silent, slow thing. His eyes stared at me the whole time, and his mouth was open wide in an attempt to gasp for air, but his lungs never inflated.

Just like his existence in the Games, his death was a boring, minuscule thing.

"Not much of a show," I muttered.

Aubrey must have sensed my disappointment. She came up to my side, her slim fingers finding my upper arm.

"I have an idea on how to make this a little more exciting."

I looked at her, a sick type of warmth filling my chest.

What can my little bloodied angel have in store for me?

The curiosity was enough to cause another round of burning need for her to rage through me.

"Show me what you got, Peaches."

Aubrey

You look like you've seen a ghost.

T hey're fucking crazy.

The type of crazy that had my stomach tingling and my thighs clenching. I wanted Cam in ways I never even thought of before.

Being with them became a need. *An obsession.*

I once thought I was alone in the world and no one would ever be able to match up to my level. Every time I played with people and toyed with the idea of being in a relationship, it always felt flat.

They turned boring. *Except Cam.* They were the complete opposite of what I had expected and continued to surprise me.

During the last few hours in the maze, it became clear, even if Cam didn't know it, that this was their world. They had the power to change people. To rule if they wanted to.

The darkness inside them was all-consuming and only showed up when they were backed into a corner. When they had a show to put on. A fucked-up, bloody show that would have the people outside know *exactly* what family they came from.

And I'm honored to take part in it.

I took a step back, my masterpiece finally coming together.

My watch lit up, pings filling the air.

. . .

3_TOAST_BOY_5

Fuck that guy! He got wHat he deserved!

AMZYFIELDER

Crazy bitch.... Ride the cowboy again.

"Vic is going to fucking love this," I murmured with a smile.

Cam was at my side, a small huff of a laugh falling from their plump lips.

Hiram was nailed to the wall with spikes from the previous trap, blood still falling from the wounds. His face, which had slowly turned gray, and his eyes wide in fear, were surrounded by a painting in his own blood.

A clown. Complete with a twisted big smile and a large red nose.

Behind him on the wall was written, *Happy Birthday, Vic!*

It was gory. So gory. And everything I had wished for Natalie at the beginning of my time in the maze. A deplorable, embarrassing end that would forever go down in the game's history.

I'm going to make history. Alongside Cam.

Children would look back on our Games, watch our live streams in detail. Try to recreate what we had done for years to come. They would know who we were.

My fame wasn't just limited to my after-dark channel anymore.

The Aubrey that came into the Games with the intention of killing her archnemesis from high school seemed so far in the past that it was almost hard to believe we were the same person.

That Aubrey was hell-bent on getting her enemy and not stopping until she felt satisfied. She probably would have gone after Hiram if it wasn't for a certain thembo cowboy hauling her ass out of the way as water rushed toward them.

But they did. They grabbed me by the hand and—*literally*— swept me off my feet. Up until then, not a single person had blown me away like they did.

Had excited me the way they did. And ultimately put me in my place like they did.

And fuck, I enjoyed being put in my place.

They knew what I needed, desired, and they weren't afraid to give it to me.

"Good job, Peaches," they praised. A thrill ran through me at the tone of their voice. The feeling of their hand slapping my clit still fresh in my mind had a shiver running up my spine.

Fuck. How did I get so lucky to run into this fucked-up thembo cowboy? For the first time in my life, I truly felt *lucky*.

I hadn't met Cam because of my own skill or because of something I could control. It had been all them.

They had single-handedly changed the trajectory of how the Games were supposed to go for me. Fuck, if I was being honest, they changed the trajectory of my whole life.

Even when we got out of the maze, there was no going back. They had tattooed themselves on my heart, there was no getting rid of me or the bond we had forged.

"Welcome to the dark side," I said and threaded my fingers through theirs. "Glad to finally see the real you."

Their smile had my heart skipping a beat. I wondered if they knew how tightly they had me wrapped around their finger.

"I've always been here, darlin'," they said and pulled me closer. They had to lean down to brush their lips across mine. "Are you ready to win this thing?"

I ran my hands up their muscled arms. I wanted to do so much more. I didn't give two fucks about winning. I wanted to hole up in the maze and fuck them until I forgot my own name.

They were the only person that ever brough *that* level of pleasure to me. I wanted more of it. Wanted to see what they would do once I was all theirs. No camera. No audience. No death game.

Would they let the darkness loose if they knew no one was watching? Would they whorship me or would they degrade me?

A shiver ran through my body.

The need to please them was something I'd never felt before.

I wasn't stupid. I knew more sponsors would come from this. That Cam and I would be set. Prize money aside, companies were going to bounce at the opportunity to have *the* maze duo promote their shit.

But the real world meant nothing to me anymore. Sure, the money would be nice. So would the attention and sponsorships. But it would be nothing without *them*. There was nothing more exciting waiting for me out there than the continuation of my life with them.

All I needed was right there in front of me. And I was never going to let Cam go. They were stuck with me, and if they ever even thought about leaving me, I would make both of our lives, and those of whoever dared interfere, a living hell.

Not just that. I would *kill* whoever dared take them. Slit their throat and gut them before dropping them off at Cam's doorstep so they would know how serious I was about them.

I didn't need to say any of that. Cam knew it. They knew just how much I was willing to do for them.

But for Cam, winning the Games was everything they had set out to do, and with it so close, there was no way I'd be ruining it for them. We could focus on everything else *after*. Because there would be an after. *We* would have an after... whatever that looked like.

So I wrapped my arms around them instead and said, "You know it, cowboy."

And sealed it with a kiss.

It was oddly quiet in the lead up to the finish line.

The only sounds were our footsteps and slightly labored breathing.

We'd been stuck in the maze for hours. We killed multiple people—well, I did at least. We'd been betrayed, hurt, almost boiled, almost drowned.

The tiredness was wearing on us both.

My limbs were heavy, dragging me to the ground with each step I took. The only thing keeping me from stopping for a break was Cam's desire to win. For them, I would keep going.

Even if my thighs screamed at me to stop. Even if my energy was sucked from me after the brutal orgasms they had given me. Even if the sweat had caused my makeup to run and my clothes were dirty and torn. Even if I wasn't wearing panties anymore.

It's all worth it.

We had been walking for maybe twenty minutes when we turned a corner, and right in front of us was an opening out of the maze. No one had come after us, and there were no signs of any other players in the vicinity.

Maybe they all died.

Or maybe the Architects had set this up just for us as a reward for giving them the show of a lifetime.

It was like a beacon. Beckoning us closer. It looked so *easy*.

That should have been my first red flag.

But I was just too tired to notice.

Bright lights shone through the opening, creating a break in the fluorescent lighting of the covered, concrete maze.

It's asking us to run to it. To make a break for it because, in just a few steps, victory would be ours.

I could taste it on my tongue. Feel the cool air slap against my heated face.

But this wasn't the only path leading out.

There were two more openings leading to the main exit. The hallways were dark but still noticeably empty.

As soon as we stepped around the corner, screams rang out.

Excited, loud, ear-ringing screams. It was such a jarring noise after walking in dead silence for so long.

Like most years, the audience and press run were right outside the finish line. They would get to see the first and last of the contestants to make it through.

Whoever was first would have their photos splattered across all social media channels and news outlets.

My guess was that it was used to motivate the players. Just like the finish line at the end of a marathon, loved ones would be waiting for you and would celebrate when you won.

But this was far more fucked up, especially for the families that had to watch as one bloodied player after the next made it out of the maze, while their loved one was left inside to be taken care of by the clean-up crew, never to be seen alive again save for the replays of that year's maze.

How pitiful. To only be remembered by how flashy your death was.

But that was the name of the game.

And it would happen for Ella. For Natalie. For Hiram.

They were dead. The only thing keeping their memory alive were the ghosts of them on every maze stream thereafter. Their "best moments" would be replayed over and over again until even their family members got desensitized.

"Wait, help me fix my makeup," I said, pulling Cam back with a jerk.

They let out an annoyed huff, but it was twinged with playfulness. They turned to me, their hands running through my hair before their fingers swiped the sides of my lips and eyes.

I leaned into their hand, enjoying the warmth that seeped into my skin.

I'm down bad.

And it was clear for all to see. But I didn't give a shit. I would take everything Cam was willing to give me. No matter how little.

I was reveling in the attention... until I saw a flash behind them.

I had only moments to react, but I knew if I didn't, Cam might be lost to me forever. It was pure instinct. The way my body and mind synced together within as little as a second to protect them.

Protect them. Something I never wanted to do for even a moment in my life. Never had I wanted to *sacrifice* my safety for someone else.

It wasn't who I was. I protected myself first and foremost. *Always.* Because no one else stuck their neck out for me, so I was forced to do it myself.

Except for Cam. Cam had been there for me throughout the entire maze, even when their life was at stake.

And now I'm returning the favor.

I placed both my hands on their chest and shoved them as hard as I could. Not expecting it, they stumbled back, their eyes widening.

Fire burst out from either side of the wall, cutting a path between the two of us. Bright red and orange filled my vision, blocking most of Cam's figure from view. When another burst went off behind me, I gasped and turned around, the sound of my hair sizzling hitting my ear.

So fucking close.

Flames were raging around me, licking at my skin. It was incredibly hot, burning me and causing my outfit to stick to me.

Just like previous years.

I should have prepared better. Should have known that a straight shot to the end was too good to be true.

But in previous years, the contestants were often alone. *I wasn't.* Not only that, but I was with Cam, and I had the utmost trust that they would get me out of it.

I couldn't make out anything, a red haze covering my vision. The panic I felt made my breath quicken, causing me to inhale more heat, more smoke. Intense fear clawed at my throat.

I hugged my torso, trying to make my body as small as possible.

Breathe in and out.

But I couldn't. The heat went straight into my lungs, burning on its way down and forcing a cough from me.

It wasn't until I turned back to Cam that I realized the flames were crawling across the floor of the concrete maze, inching closer and closer to me. There was no way out. No lever to stop them from overtaking me.

I'm going to die.

It became clear in the few moments I had.

I had been lucky to make it through the trap floor, but this trap seemed designed to kill. The Architects had wanted there to be one last bang before crossing the finish line.

And they sure fucking got one.

"Cam—"

My voice died when I saw that Cam wasn't even looking at me. No, they were staring back at the exit where the finish line was.

Just over the flames, I could make out a familiar face.

Elijah. That fucking bastard. He was smiling at them as his back stood facing the exit.

"What's wrong? You look like you've seen a ghost?" His crazy laughter echoed through the hallway.

"Cam," I called, panic edging my voice as the flames grew closer. "Please find the switch."

They wouldn't fucking dare.

When they took a step forward, my heart fucking shattered.

I had never experienced a betrayal more powerful than I felt in that moment. It crushed my heart. Felt like I was falling through the trapdoor all over again, knocking the air out of my lungs.

It hurt. Even more than the fire licking at my skin and the heat crowding my lungs.

How can they do this to me?

Realistically, I knew that the people who entered the maze were all fucked up and would probably throw someone under the bus to save themselves. Fuck, I was one of them. But foolishly, I had thought Cam was different. That I could believe their words. Their actions.

Are you ready to win this thing? They had wanted to bring me across the finish line with them. But the more I watched them and Elijah, the more frightened I got.

Don't leave me.

I wanted to say it, but the words weren't coming out of my mouth. Like my brain didn't want to fully come to terms with what was happening.

Even if the fire threatened to end me.

They took another step.

Cam, don't you leave me!

They took *another* and *another*, all without looking back.

And then I finally found my voice.

"Cam, don't you fucking leave me here, you cunt!"

CAM

Aubrey's panicked voice was ringing in my ears, but not louder than Pa's voice.

No! Leave the girl! Take the win! Take what's yours! Take it! Take it! Take it!

I wouldn't let Elijah take this from me. All those who were part of the Ranch lived there, received an education there; we talked, played together when we were children. We were closer than just random players in the maze. Back at the Ranch, he was like a brother to me. But the moment he stepped foot into the arena at the same time as me—once he'd made his offering—that didn't mean a hill of beans. He was just another fuckin' obstacle.

And it would be the same for anyone else who entered the maze, whether they were Ranch or not. He isn't special.

I repeated that in my head.

Elijah isn't special.

He's nobody.

The lick of flames made sweat dew along my skin, the oppressive heat bitin' into me even from the safety that Aubrey had created in her sacrifice.

There wasn't any time to hesitate. I had a choice to make.

Win or lose. The end was so close. The cool air from outside hit my front, the flames licked my back. I just had to choose which one I wanted *more*.

Which one I was willing to give more for.

So why did both options feel like losing?

I could leave her. Run for the exit, maybe even kill Elijah while I had the chance. The flames would consume her, burning her smooth skin and gorgeous blonde hair. Her screams would be forever replayed on the soundtrack of my win as I walked out of the maze. I'd spend the rest of my life watching the footage of me turning my back on the first thing in my life I'd ever chosen for myself.

If I left her there, if she died because I'd chased after Elijah... I'd never forgive myself. Of that I was entire certain... But was it enough to turn my back on everything I'd ever known?

It'd only been a couple hours since we first met. Since I finally got my fill of her delicious sweetness. Since I first saw just how open and willin' she was to accept the parts of me I hid deep inside.

The length of time might've been short, but the connection was undeniable.

Written in blood and ashes.

Especially when we were separated, or I saw her in danger. It was like my body and heart had a mind of their own. They'd ignored everythin' I should do in favor of savin' her.

And yet... I hesitated.

I'd entered the Games for a reason.

And if I helped her and that treacherous cunt won instead of me? I'd never be able to face it. I'd have to go back to the Ranch, my entire family and the Church watchin' as the last of the Weston line lost to one of their own brothers in faith.

A disappointment.

An embarrassment.

How would anyone still believe in the Ranch's effectiveness if their own child couldn't win the maze? If they chose failure in favour of mercy. Turned their back on the very tenets we espoused?

I'd never live it down.

My body was movin' before I'd fully made my decision, the knife that Ella'd used to threaten me finding my hand and clicking open the moment it was free of my back pocket.

Save her, or win. Are these really my only two options?

I looked back at Aubrey, barely able to make out her shape behind the flames. Her screams were loud in my ears, panic seepin' through the air to lick at me as surely as the heat.

The fear.

It hit me hard, but the sweet, cool air from the opening of the maze was beckonin' like I was a lost child and it was a house made a' candy.

I turned back to Elijah as Aubrey let out a pained moan. She'd stopped yelling at me. Stopped cursing me. Her coughs even beginning to quiet in my hesitation.

Screams and cheers were still pouring in from the opening, the sound of thousands of clapping hands roaring in my eyes. Behind me, the flames were rumbling. My own breath echoing in my ears as I faced Elijah, everything else slowly fading into the background.

"Are you comin', or what?" Elijah asked with a cheeky grin that showed off his crooked teeth. "Second place ain't so bad, Cammy."

He looked worse for wear. His face covered in blood—I wasn't sure whose—and dirt. The side of his cheek'd been split, showin' just how close he'd been to dyin' when Aubrey's trap went off.

Just like we'd been taught, he was still goin', no matter that exhaustion was pulling his shoulders down. Just like I was. We were too close to the end of the maze to stop now.

But he'd made a mistake. He'd *underestimated* me. How far I was willin' to go.

"Sorry, Eli," I called, throwin' the knife with the kind of precision that came from years of target practice. "Only one of us is crossin' that finish line."

The knife embedded itself into his eye socket, the man, hardly much older than a boy, crumplin' to the ground with a thud drowned by the roar of flames. I heard a buzz, but it didn't register either. It seemed too far away.

The weight of my decision threatened to pull me into madness, my mind heavy with the reality that I'd just betrayed my entire family.

All for a woman.

Naw, not a woman, an *angel*.

I turned, hardly able to see her through the blaze.

"Don't you worry your pretty little head, Peaches. I'm comin', sweetheart!"

The wall was entirely smooth, save for the gaps where the flames were comin' from, the metal glowing red with heat. But I knew there had to be... somethin'. A valve. A puzzle. A way to turn it off.

Aubrey coughed out of my sight, the smoke and heat long since overwhelmed her. The noise made my brain rattle in my skull, panic makin' my movements jerky as I felt over the walls and floor desperately for somethin', anythin'.

Like a fuckin' raccoon digging for garbage.

And then I heard it. My watch came to life, and I knew now the last buzz I'd heard was my PK... But now? It'd gotta be somethin' else.

Ping!

Vic_Official: *look up!*

My eyes traveled upwards, spotting the metal hook hangin' from the ceiling above the center of the blaze.

I'd only have one shot at this. If I missed, my rope would fall into the flames, and Aubrey would be burned to a crisp.

I unhooked the lasso from my side, rotating the rope a few times before aimin' it straight for the hook.

Seconds slowed into hours as I watched my throw fly, the fibers catchin' around the metal. I pulled hard, and water exploded from the ceiling, rainin' down and extinguishin' the flames.

Lord be DAMNED, I am sick of being wet!

Butit didn't mean shit the moment Aubrey came into view, singed and curled into a ball in the middle of the floor, deep black marks on the hot, cracked stones. The soles of my boots stuck slightly to the floor where they'd begun to melt as I lifted her into my arms in a sort of bridal carry, careful not to jostle her too hard.

"Peaches? You hang in there for me angel. Cam's got you now."

She groaned, and I thanked my lucky stars for the noise as she begun to stir, the thick drops of water clearing the soot from her face in streaks.

"Cam?" she whispered softly, her hand fistin' in the fabric of my soggy tank top.

"Right here," I murmured, heading for the exit, the cool air and noise floodin' back with every step.

Camera flashes were damn near blinding as I turned sideways, ensuring that Aubrey and I stepped through into the winners circle at the same time to a roar of cheers and applause. The people were ravenous. Hands reached out to try and touch us. Paparazzi were screaming our names evey which direction.

A fucking madhouse. I had been on the other side, watching my siblings make it through, but never had I imagined it be *that* jarring.

After the relative quiet of the arena it was overwhelming. The sights and sounds a dizzyin' array of sensations that left me feelin' off-kilter. I squeezed my eyes shut briefly, taking a deep breath and focusin' on the fragile body in my arms.

"Cam?" My head turned at Pa's familiar southern drawl, his thick moustache practically quivering with rage as our eyes locked. Luckily there was a small fence and about a thousand cameras or he might just teach me a lesson right then and there. "What in Heaven have you done?"

My lip curled, the anger that'd been bubblin' since the moment I'd seen Elijah boiling over the blackened kettle of my emotions. Pa choosing to send him in gave a message, and I read it loud and fucking clear.

He never trusted me. He never thought I'd live up to the family name.

I hadn't realized until that moment. Where Pa stood behind that fence, eyes enraged, jaw tight, fists clenched, that he had instilled so much hatred in me.

I used to look up to him. To the family. But that changed ever since enterin' the maze. Ever since he sent Elijah in with me.

There was no going back. I chose my side.

And I'm damn fucking proud of it.

"Made a show of it," I snarled triumphantly, spitting at his feet. "Now if you'll fuckin' excuse me, traitor, I have a podium to get to."

VICTORIA

NEGOTIATIONS ARE FOR PEOPLE WHO READ THE FINE PRINT.

Kohl's lips trailed along my inner thigh, nibbling and kissing along the sensitive skin and making me squirm. My face tilted backwards, eyes sliding away from their golden hair to the ceiling, the back of my head meeting the cool glass pane of the mirror.

"Will you permit me to taste you, goddess?" they asked, mouth moving into the crease of my thigh for a seductive suck that made my knees tremble under the weight of my urgent need for them.

Something about seeing Hiram torn to shreds that had me slick and panting, waiting to be freed from the chains of the anchor's desk so that we could *finally* have a moment alone. There was a lot to catch up on, after all.

"Yes," I murmured, a hand grabbing their short hair to control them, moving their mouth where I sorely needed it against my wet, aching center. "I love you, my little slut."

It was true, had been true for a long time. But it was a relief that I'd finally gotten the chance to tell them.

Kohl's strong hands spread my thighs further, my short skirt bunching around my waist. I'd ditched my underwear the moment we'd gotten back in the dressing room, pushing aside cosmetics to make room for myself atop the vanity. The hot lights were an exciting addition—warming my back and threatening that, if I leaned too far back, I was sure to be burned.

But the mirror? That was nostalgic. Reminding me of the way Khol had thrown me into the glass, the shards raining down on us as I fought for my life against my would-be murderer. Under their shirt, hidden by nothing more than a bit of cotton—polyester if i was being serious—was a scabbed *V*.

A testament of their worship of me, rivaled only by the magic they were working with their mouth.

Kohl licked at my slit, the flat of their tongue traveling to collect my sticky arousal with a hum of pleasure. Their fingers bit into my thighs, short nails digging into the skin as they devoured me. Desperate to help get my mind off what had been an exceptionally stressful day.

"Good boy, kitten," I praised, a moan slipping through my parted lips. "Make your goddess come..."

Kohl's lips closed around my clit, sucking firmly and making my eyes roll. Their fingers teased my needy, twitching hole as they continued to slurp at my cunt like they were starved for it.

"Fuck me," I commanded, hips canting against their face in a clear demand. "Now, Kohl."

Kohl groaned, their fingers sliding inside and arching, aiming for my sweet spot. The move was successful, my knees trying to draw together around their head as my pleasure increased, threatening to throw me over the edge. I'd just about given in to the waves of my need when the door swung open without so much as a knock, a woman entering with the click of her lacquered stilettos and a raised eyebrow.

The men at her side, clearly hired muscle, leered as they caught sight of Kohl kneeling between my legs.

"Do you fucking mind?" I snapped, pushing Kohl's face further against me as they tried to pull away. "I didn't tell *you* to stop," I hissed at them, meeting the disgusted eyes of the woman evenly. "And I don't remember telling you to come in either."

It likely would've been more impressive if I hadn't moaned in the middle of my sentence, but they were the ones interrupting, not me.

"Can you please make yourself decent?" the woman, a producer named Sarah-Beth with mousy brown hair and thin lips, asked.

I rolled my eyes, releasing Kohl's hair and letting them come up for air. Their little gasp to catch their breath was music to my ears.

"Prude," they muttered, continuing to finger me like we hadn't been interrupted. Their mouth finding the soft flesh of my inner thigh for a sharp nip.

"I suggest you avert your eyes if you want to keep them," I snapped at the guard. "Seriously, SB, you needed to bring goons with you to relieve us of our duties? You are such a puss—"

"Relieve you?" Sarah-Beth scoffed, taking a stylus from behind her ear to mark something carelessly on her tablet. "No, no, why would I be doing that?"

"Because we fulfilled our agreement," Kohl said, their eyes flashing up to mine for reassurance. "We're done here."

"Exactly," I murmured, moving my skirt to cover myself—not that it did much good with Kohl's lithe hands moving inside me and making it hard to concentrate. That edge that I'd been chasing returned quickly with their thumb rubbing little circles against my clit, the wet sound of their fingers fucking me punctuating my sentences. "We're done here," I echoed.

"Maybe before you pulled that little stunt with Hiram." Sarah-Beth tsked. "Really couldn't help yourself, could you? If you'd just stuck to the script, you wouldn't be in this mess, you know?"

I scoffed, my mood souring as Kohl removed their fingers from inside me, their glistening digits making their way between their lips as they turned their head to glare at the woman.

"We're done here," I repeated, firmer this time.

"No, you aren't. Get suited up. The game is about to start."

"We're not playing in anymore fucking *games*." My voice rose now as I slid off the vanity and to the floor with a thud of my boots. "We made our money, made you your money. Now it's time for us to go."

"About that..." Sarah-Beth started, a ferocious, eerily excited gleam in her hooded eyes. "I regret to inform you that your contract was violated by inciting violence and failing to be impartial to all competitors." She fake-frowned, her overlined lips pulling downwards in a mocking pout. "Sorry about that."

It was clear to me that was a load of shit, clear to Kohl too as he jerked up from the floor to lunge at her, making the woman stumble backwards in her heels, her tight pencil skirt nearly making her topple over.

They would've gotten to her too if her bodyguard hadn't moved to block them, catching Kohl's shoulder with a massive, ham-sized fist.

"Ah ah ah," she said, voice lowering into a hiss. "We can either do this the easy way, Victoria, or we can do it the hard way."

"And if I choose not to do it at all?"

"Well, if you'd like to see your little buddy here in a body bag, that's an option, princess."

My eyes flicked to Kohl, their arm being held perilously behind their back. Smart of them to go after my partner, even if it set my teeth on edge. It's what I would've done in their position. Manipulate my weak point.

The seconds ticked by as I glowered furiously.

There was no real choice here, not if they were going to hurt Kohl.

"That's what I thought," Sarah-Beth cooed with a syrupy smile. "Now, get dressed. We need to get you back into hair and makeup."

"For what?" Kohl asked with a huff as they were released, brushing themselves off and flexing their fingers.

"Truth or Dare, obviously." Sarah-Beth replied, ticking off something else on her tablet.

Kohl's eyes met mine, wide and anxious. My lip curled furiously—the only one who got that reaction out of them was me.

"Why the fuck would we do that? We're rich as shit as it is, no reason to sign up."

"Hm, about that. Go off script, no cash. Didn't you read the contract you signed?"

I opened my mouth to argue, but she put her hand up to stop me.

"We aren't *monsters*, Victoria. Win Truth or Dare, and you can keep whatever money you earn in the game—and we'll pay you your contract amount too."

"I—"

"I'm going to remind you that we aren't really asking."

I chewed the inside of my cheek to stop myself from insulting her, the injustice of it all weighing me down.

The idea of walking back into that arena? Of having to watch Kohl walk in there with me?

I'd rather drop dead.

"Fine, but we have stipulations."

"Negotiations are for people who read the fine print," Sarah-Beth reminded me. "Get dressed. Game starts in a few hours."

We didn't want to play the first time, much less twice.

And here we were, staring down re-entry into the arena like it was the barrel of a gun. It practically was. The thing about Truth or Dare was that it was a game of secrets. And who had more secrets than Legacies? Worse, Legacies whose parents became *Architects*.

Seventy-two hours earlier, I would've laughed this off. What kind of secrets could they have dug up to use to blackmail me with, really?

Now?

I was terrified of what else they'd manage to find.

If Kohl and I managed to survive the game, would our relationship?

"Fine," I hissed, catching Kohl's eye.

The TV was still playing highlights of Cam and Aubrey's win.

Speaking of new relationships and nothing to lose, I had an idea.

Sarah's balding crony delivered a punishing punch to Kohl's ribs, making them double over onto their hands and knees with a wheeze.

The moment they left the room, Sarah-Beth tapping her watch like a fucking cunt, I raced to Kohl, catching their face in my hand.

"You okay?"

"Fine," they spat out irritably. "You had your scheming face on. Have a plan?"

"When don't I?" I asked breezily, helping them stand. "They really think they can play us like this? Fuck us over and we are just going to take it? As if. Bring in the fucking crazies."

"The crazies?" they asked in bewilderment, rubbing their ribs.

I reached out to grip their chin, turning their head toward Aubrey and Cam, waving and smiling for the cameras.

"About time we go congratulate our old friend Aubrey, don't you think?"

Maybe Cam was onto something about this winning thing.

Looking out onto the crowd of people, all of them vying for our photo, yelling questions, and overall just treating us like stars was something I'd never experienced in my life.

My after-dark channel had some similar perks along with my sponsorships, but standing here was... *enlightening.*

They absolutely loved us. Some of them looked at us like we were gods.

I mean, we sort of are.

In the maze, *we* chose who lived or died. *We* were the ones who'd stopped Elijah from winning. Collected Hiram's prize money. Had the most viewership. Held them all in the palm of our hands. Baited breaths waiting at the edge of their seats.

Sounds pretty fucking godlike to me.

I stood straight, trying to ignore the pain traveling through my body form the burns and cuts littering my skin. The after-game medics were great and had dressed my wounds almost as soon as the photo-op at the maze exit was over, but that didn't mean I was miraculously healed.

It'd been hours since we first stepped into the maze. I'd run for my life, fell from a hole to a shallow, water-filled concrete floor, gotten the life fucked out of me, and almost got burned to a crisp. Tired didn't even begin to cover it.

I'm ready to get the fuck out of here.

Natalie's face flashed across my mind. I'd almost forgotten her when Cam entered my life. The way her death was ripped from my hands by Hiram... It hardly seemed like it mattered anymore.

Maybe I should thank her.

As annoying as she fucking had been, she'd also been the reason I entered the Games in the first place. And without entering the maze, I would've never met Cam.

The thought was almost enough to make me cringe.

"Thank you," Cam whispered as we did our obligatory photo-op on the winners' podium. Their voice sending warm tendrils of electricity down my spine. It was painful having to stand there for all the paparazzi and Devil's Playground photographers to get their fill when we should've been somewhere private enjoying a moment just the two of us.

At the very least, I wanted to thank them properly for saving my life, for choosing me.

What should've been five minutes ran on twenty, then thirty.

Cam's family had left after the blowout, but they seemed like they were surprisingly okay with it. Maybe even a bit lighter, standing tall with their shoulders back proudy for the cameras.

There was no one for me in the audience. The only person I wanted to see was Vic, but God only knew what she was doing after the Games.

I still need to thank her for all the help she gave us. Who knows what we would've done if she hadn't given us that hint?

I turned to Cam, raised an eyebrow at their lopsided, giddy grin.

"Did you hit your head on the way out or something?"

They looked even better under the winners' spotlight, if that was even possible. Their golden tan skin still slick with a sheen of sweat and dried blood, their hair slightly matted and sticking up at odd angles. It was chaotic, messy.

I absolutely loved it.

I want to lick each and every inch of their muscular arms.

This earned me a chuckle from them, their lips turning into a sensual smile. A hand found my lower back, drawing me closer to a flurry of erratic camera flashes.

"You kept your promise," they said, dark eyes trailing my body. "You helped me reach my goal."

They took my hand, drawing it to their lips to place a kiss against my knuckles. It was such a simple gesture, incredibly tame in comparison to the rough fucking I'd ensured in the maze, but had my heart absolutely pounding. I didn't even know I had the energy left for it to race like it did.

"After we get this grime off us, I'm gonna fuck you so hard you forget everyone you've ever been with before me," I vowed.

This earned me a laugh, Cam's sharp canine teeth catching the light.

"First the after party, Peaches," they said. "Then I'm all yours for the takin'."

"What happened to *after* the party?" I asked against Cam's lips as they pushed us into an empty room, their hands pushing the short skirt of my dress up to my waist.

"No one asked you to wear this dress, Peaches," they muttered through kisses.

The dress in question was skintight pink pleather and hugged my body. It was so tight that I couldn't even wear any underwear under it. Much less move normally.

Honestly? It was a bit of a relief to have my thighs freed from their sweaty, pleather prison.

Cam took my new found mobility as the perfect opportunity to push me against the wall, fall to their knees, and stick their face between my legs.

They grabbed two handfuls of my ass and forced my cunt to their mouth.

I gasped as their tongue ran along my folds.

"Is this my *real* thank you?" I asked, my hips jerking against their face.

They hummed against me as they took my clit into their mouth for a heady *suck*. It absolutely sent me spinning, my hand tangling in their hair and forcing them closer.

Unlike in the maze, it was just me and them.

For the first time, I wasn't getting fucked for the camera. It was just the two of us in here. Strangely, I felt even more vulnerable than when millions of people were watching.

With the stream, I could hide how I felt through overexaggerated moans and expressions, but with them, I couldn't. They pulled orgasms out of me with ease and left me writhing with even the simplest of touches.

They *controlled* me. And that was hard to get used to when I'd spent my entire life in control of everything I laid my eyes on.

Unable to take being worshiped, I tugged them up and forced their lips back to mine. They didn't fight me, the unspoken request between us loud and clear.

I moaned at the taste of myself on them.

My hand slipped into their suit pants, my fingers coming into contact with wetness.

They groaned against me, their hand coming to rub circles against my clit. Heat unfurled in my belly, my beat-up body feeling like it'd been dunked into a warm bath as my muscles began to loosen at their coaxing touch.

"We don't have much time," I breathed. "Better make this fucking worth it."

They laughed against me before their other hand grabbed the hair at the base of my neck and forced my head back.

"Like you fuckin' care about time. Keep goin'," they commanded against my neck, their teeth dragging across the sensitive skin.

I was so taken off guard by their quickness that I forgot what I was doing, but I quickly remedied my mistake and began rubbing hard, fast circles on their clit, pulling a few good moans from them.

I teased their folds before pushing two fingers inside. They did the same to me, both of us writhing against each other as we played.

It should've been illegal how fast Cam made me come. Little stars bursting at the corners of my vision as I fucked myself on their hand.

Honestly, it was downright embarrassing.

But when my pussy clenched and a tingling heat started from my core and moved outward, I didn't complain.

Cam was groaning against me, their movements becoming erratic. Breathing heavy against my neck, and every so often they biting down on my skin, sucking and nipping along my throat.

I hope to God they leave marks.

I came in an explosion of heat, not too unlike the fire I was trapped between in the maze. After all the craziness and barely making it out alive, the orgasm Cam gave me felt like the strongest, most mind-blowing one I'd ever felt. Leaving my legs trembling under my weight and forcing me to lean heavily against the wall of support.

And they didn't even fucking do much.

"Come for me, cowboy."

The simple command did it. They fell into me as their cunt clenched my fingers in waves, shudders running through their body as they came. Their hand tightened in my hair like they were worried I'd leave.

I wouldn't. There was no leaving. They were mine, and I was theirs.

Of that, I was sure of.

They pulled away, a huge smile on their breathless face interrupted by their fingers as they removed them from inside of me and popped them into their mouth to suck them clean.

"*Fucking delicious*," they groaned, dropping their hand to my waist to crowd me further against the wall. "Do y'know how tempted I was to get on my knees for you after tasting that bat?"

"I bet we taste even better together," I said with a wicked smile.

Instead of bringing my fingers to my mouth, I forced them into theirs. Cam sucked, tongue rolling around the digits as their eyes narrowed in bliss.

"Fuck, I don't know how much more I can take. I need you in every way possi—"

"Clear the room!"

A pounding caught our attention and had us both turning to the door.

Anger ran through me. *Can't they leave us alone? We won, for fuck's sake.* The killer urges from the maze still hadn't fully disappeared, and I was ready to smash someone's brain in for even daring to look at us the wrong way. Much less outright interrupt our privacy.

"I guess we gotta make a show of it," Cam said, sending me a look that told me to cool it.

With a pout, I pushed past them, pulling down my insanely tight dress as I walked.

When I pushed open the door, one of the guards Devil's Playground employed to watch the winners was waiting outside with a scowl.

"Ten minutes is up," he said and motioned for us to get out. "You're lucky I even gave you that much."

I opened my mouth to say something that would've no doubt ruined his day, but Cam was there, their heavy arm over my shoulder in seconds.

"You got it," they said and pushed us both out of the room and back into the party.

There was a reason I left it in the first place, and it wasn't just to fuck Cam.

It was overwhelming at best. It wasn't just the winners who got invited, but also the top twenty contestants, various media outlets, Devil's Playground higher-ups, previous winners and some randos that had connections with the Games. All of us were forced into a large penthouse that overlooked the area. It was one of the only livable buildings on the island and was reserved for only the most high-profile people in the Games. A sort of box suite to enjoy the Games from.

The lights were dim, music was blasting, drugs were flowing. And there we were, forced to stay and 'enjoy' it.

At least they cleaned us up first. I was worried that they would have me parading around in my dried, bloody outfit to make it more interesting.

"Just a few more hours," Cam whispered in my ear, their hand rubbing soothing circles on my shoulder. "And then I'll have my face between your legs again, Peaches."

I shivered at their tone.

"Well, the least we can do is get fucked up," I said and grabbed two drinks from a server that happened to be passing by. I acted like I was giving it to Cam, but as soon as they reached for it, I jerked it back and downed it.

"Brat," they said and reached for the other, but I pulled that one away two.

"Oh, sorry, did I say we?" I asked with a raised brow. "I meant me since I helped you win and all."

They let out an irritated chuckle that warmed my body. "You're beggin' for a lesson in manners."

"You did good, you little psychopath."

My head swiveled around toward the familiar voice.

Vic stood with her arms crossed and a slight smile on her face, Kohl just behind her shoulder, looking anxious to be in a room so full of people.

I let out an excited squeal and threw my arms around Vic. She let out a laugh but returned my hug, even if her movementions were hesitant.

That's fine, she'd always been prickly.

"I knew you'd like it! Oh my god look at your *hair*!" I said and pulled away to look at her. "What are you doing here? Lemme guess, divvying up my prize money?"

It was meant as a joke, but there was no humor in Vic's face. She looked back at Kohl, who'd been surveying the area, their eyes falling over every single guard before turning back to her and giving her a nod.

"There's something bigger happening. We need to go back in," Vic said, her voice dropping to a whisper. "I don't have time to explain all the fucked-up shit that's happened, but I need help."

Vic needs help? Out of all the people in the world, Vic would be the last to ask for help from anyone.

"Anything," I replied quickly.

Cam was by my side, a possessive hand on the small of my back. Vic's eyes flitted to them, then back to me. Kohl stepped closer, the tension rising.

"Do you trust me?" Vic asked.

"Always. Whatever you need."

She gave a stiff nod.

"I need you to go back in. I need you to enter Truth or Dare with us."

My heart skipped a beat in my chest. If it were anyone else, I would turn it down immediately. I had no reason to join the Games. I didn't want money or fame.

But for a friend...

"Well," I hedged, giving her a beaming smile. "I have nothing else planned." I turned to Cam, who was looking at me with an expression I couldn't decipher. "Are you coming?"

Truth and Dare was more personal than the Maze. A bunch of people put together to have their secrets exposed while millions watched. Cam would learn things about me, I would learn things about them. Dangerous, dark things.

Maybe they won't like you anymore once they find out.

I pushed the thought away as Cam gave me their award-winning smile.

"You're crazier than a bedbug if you think I'm letting you go in there alone," they said and pulled me closer, distrust in their eyes as they touched on Kohl.

I leaned into them and looked back at Vic with a smile. "Play hard."

She offered her hand, which I took immediately to shake. "Win, win."

Trix

Welcome, players, to Truth or Dare.

Time always moved faster when it was the least convenient. Like a days somehow had a few hours less than I anticipated.

I ran into my room, locking the door behind me. Not that it would do my much good, the cheap stock door was hollow, the lock barely strong enough to hold up to a couple kicks. It'd be mere minutes until they were inside and forcing me to the ground. Still, the little action calmed me. There was a process to these things. An order.

I need to act fast.

My heart was pounding, making it difficult to concentrate. Beads of sweat dripped down the back of my neck and dampened the collar of my shirt, cooling steadily and leaving an unpleasant slick chilly feeling behind.

I took steady breaths, reminding myself that I knew what I was doing. I didn't have to panic. I just had to *do* it.

But *doing* was the hardest part. I was a planner to my core. An over-analyzer. Better suited as the brainy computer loving side-kick than the sporty, go-getter hero.

And *this*? It was the gamble of a fucking lifetime.

I rummaged through my dresser drawer, pulling out the repurposed altoid's tin—covered in black duct tape and marked with a white paint marker with a skull and cross bones—and shoved it into my bra.

Was it totally necessary to make it aesthetic? No. Did I do it anyway? Yeah.

I'd been working on the damn thing for months, the least I could do was make it seem at least a little cool when I finally revealed it. Truth or Dare was a game as much as the others, and, if anything, it was even *more* focused on appearance.

My clothing was constricting, my breathing shallow as I fought to keep my cool. Turned out—much to my reluctant disapproval—that simply telling yourself to relax didn't mean that your body would agree to.

I crossed the room to my desk, pulling out another small pack, which I put in my underwear. It was small enough that it would go unnoticed, even if they decided to strip me.

I just needed to be careful.

I got this. I've been over this a hundred times. No, a thousand. This shit was air tight. Foolproof.

A loud boom told me they'd already made it through the front door.

Showtime.

I pulled the top drawer open just slightly and left it there like a beacon to whomever would come search my room after I was gone. My laptop had already been wiped, but I made a show of smashing the screen anyway. Better they waste their time trying to get into it to find fuck all than actually determine what it was that I was trying to do.

And then I waited. The sound of thunderous footsteps coming up the stairs enough to drown out the blood rushing in my ears.

I counted the seconds in my head.

One.

Two.

Three.

Fou—*BANG!*

The door gave almost instantly. Not a surprise, but a bit of a bummer. I was hoping just for a little bit more time before the five men in black were filtering into my bedroom, hardly even glancing at the posters of scantily clad women lining my walls.

Click. The unmistakable noise of five loaded guns cocking as they were pointed at me should've been terrifying. Would've been, if I didn't know that the last thing they wanted to do was actually *kill* me.

Fuck, they came prepared.

Hands reached for me, masked faces blending together as I fought them, enough to seem like I was actually afraid. And, in part, *I was.* But not hard enough to warrant being knocked out.

I screamed, kicked and spat all the way downstairs and out of the empty house. Devoid of any furniture or personal items, save for my bedroom that I'd left as a sort of shrine.

Or maybe a serial killer's murder room.

There was an unmarked van waiting for me, it's sliding door swung wide into darkness.

Didn't really matter who'd send these cunts anyway, they were either Devil's Playground, Government or the Company.

If I was honest, it was the same monster in different clothes anyway.

Night had fallen, so there was no one out to watch as the men took me kicking and screaming out of my house. They could do what they wanted, but I wasn't going to make it easy for them by going quietly. Not that it fucking mattered, the cowardly dickheads I called neighbors didn't even have the guts to peek through their curtains.

I wanted them to. I wanted the whole world to see what they were doing. But that just wasn't the neighborhood we lived in. Wasn't the society we lived in. If anything, their eyes were probably glued to the screen to watch Hide n' Seek.

The people around me were scared. Cowardly. They would

never step in if they knew their lives were at risk. And for good reason, I guess. Most people weren't into the idea of being forced into a murder game. Or prison.

Honestly, if I was given the choice, I didn't know what I'd pick either.

Many of them vocally aired their disgust for the Games. But they were the same ones who watched it in their rooms at night when they thought no one knew. The glow of screens behind closed curtains told me that.

The men pushed me into the back of the van with so much force, I barely had a chance to hold my hands out to soften the blow. I tried to grab onto the opening, but they saw what I was doing and forced my hands to my side.

I'd expected the typical fabric or leather seats of a civilian vehicle, my back and hips aching as I was forced to sit on a cold, hard metal bench lining one side of the van, its twin sister against the opposite wall as hands forced me to stay put. Cold, metal snapped tightly around my wrists, the chain between them clipped to another that was bolted to the floor.

Fucking shit damn it.

With nowhere to go and no real chance of escape, I surveyed the people there, chest heaving with the effort to force air back into my lungs.

Turns out that screaming that long, while also fighting like hell was harder work than I thought.

Two helpers and one man off to the side. They were all wearing the same all-black outfits, like some type of wannabe SWAT team. Silver threading through the top of his rapidly thinning hair, a dinged up left ear that was missing a chunk from when it was grazed by a stray bullet in the maze—*he* was the obvious leader and a person I'd researched well.

Daimen Fox.

The other two were insignificant, bullet fodder on the off chance I'd decided to really try and fight my way out of this.

Daimen was an Architect for a while before he became an over compensated lapdog to the top of the top. He appeared to be as fit as his social media profiles boasted, but without the carefully selected filters and good lighting it was obvious that he was aging after so many years on the job. Wrinkles kissed the corners of his eyes, the dark circles under his eyes damn near purple.

He'd gotten complacent, thinking that some money and a nice title would save him from everything.

How fucking wrong he was. *Cunt.*

"Undress," one of the helpers said.

"I have *rights*—"

"Not here, you don't," Daimen replied, his tone harsh. "You know what's happening, don't you?"

Yep, you're taking me to partake in something I have no desire to be in.

Well, that was sort of a lie.

No, I didn't want to play in the Games. But I needed to if I wanted to find my mom.

I knew after what she'd done that they'd come for me. It was the only logical next step. Didn't make it any less annoying.

"Does your wife know what you're doing tonight, James?" I asked one of the helpers. His eyes widened when he realized I knew his name. But that's not all I knew. "You promised her you would quit. Begged her not to leave, even when you saw what it was doing to the kids. Yet you're still here and Jenny has been, what? Kicked out of her fourth school, was it? Something about recreating Hide N' Seek on the playground and bashing a kid's skull in—"

"Are you done playing?" Daimen asked in a pitiful attempt to regain my attention. "We really don't have time for this."

James remained quiet, his face turning red in uneven blotches. The truth was his wife *did* know what he was doing tonight and was quietly packing up the kids to go spend a nice long trip at her parents' cabin up in some remote woodsy area this dickhead didn't even know the name of.

Real bummer. Almost as much of a bummer as having to

leave the house that'd become my temporary home. It wasn't mine, exactly. But it wasn't not mine either, if you gave a fuck about squatters rights.

"Aw, c'mon Damien. I hadn't even gotten to Walter's gambling addiction," I said with an exaggerated pout, hooking my thumb towards him the best I could while cuffed to the floor. It wasn't as interesting as James's situation for sure, but Walter owed the wrong people *way* too much money, and they were considering holding his dog captive until he paid it back.

I might've thought Marley and Me was a drag, but it didn't mean I was heartless.

Another bummer, really.

Besides, Walter was a total loner—not a shock given his horrifying internet search history—and didn't have much besides his little tan pug.

"How is Tank by the way?" I asked him, almost cracking a smile at the way his jaw clenched.

Daimen raised an eyebrow at me. "You really think this will save you?"

"No, what I think is that it's stupid as fuck to put me in the Games with what I know," I answered, shifting on my seat in a futile attempt to try and get more comfortable.

For a second, Daimen looked like he might actually agree with me.

"Don't make this harder than it has to be," he warned.

"And you," I said and slid across the bench so I was closer to him, my arms extended awkwardly with the chain. "When you go home to your wife, don't forget to ask her if you've ever made her come as hard as I did." His face twisted in anger and this time I didn't bite my smile back. "What, you think those three-hour salon trips were really to do her hair? Three hours on a bob, Daimen. *Really?*"

Sharon wasn't really my type, but damn did that woman *love* to talk during her post orgasm cigarette.

There was a long moment of silence and I could practically hear the steam building up inside him.

"End this."

The helpers lunged at me, taking their chance to bend me to their will.

But it was too late.

A loud boom burst from outside the van. The shock of it was so strong that it had the van turning on its side.

Expecting the impact, I braced myself for the turn and, as soon as I could, had the picks I'd stowed under my tongue out to pop the locks on the handcuffs. Seven seconds later, I was pushing the back doors open and scrambling outside.

An intense, red fire licked at the sky met by a cloud of ash and smoke. My temporary home in flames due to the explosive I'd hidden in my desk drawer. All I needed was someone *just* curious enough to open it.

Sucked to be them.

No doubt an explosion that powerful would've killed anyone unlucky enough to be inside.

I reveled in the image. Let myself feel the swell of pride from killing the *bastards* that'd taken the only person I loved.

But it wasn't long until a body collided with mine and I was wrestled to the ground.

This time, they didn't hesitate to knock me out.

By the time I came to again, my head was pounding. My mouth was dry, body threatening to sink down to the floor from my slumped seated position.

The world was.. Blurry. And not in the way I would've expected from a concussion.

Fucking assholes. They'd drugged me after they knocked me out.

A disadvantage, but nothing I couldn't work with.

I blinked rapidly, trying to chase away the darkness that permeated the edges of my vision, but the involuntary fish-eye effect never left. Only when I heard shuffling next to me and I turned my head to chase it did I realize that the room we were in was pitch black.

To my side, I could make out some shadows. And then slowly, one by one, the masks of each contestant lit up. There were twenty of them in total.

When my mask finally turned on, bright green neon played at the side of my peripheral vision.

I shifted in my seat, stretching. *They didn't restrain me.* They took the time to knock me out and drug me, but not restraining me meant they didn't give two fucks about what I did to the other contestants.

Taking stock of my body, I felt around my arms and legs to see if anything was broken or sprained. I had some bumps and bruises, but as far as I could tell they hadn't even bothered to strip me in the end, likely running behind due to the little surprise that I'd set up in my old room.

They hadn't even thought to look in my bra or underwear, I could still feel the press of the metal containers against my skin, long since heated to body temperature.

A screen lit in front of the group, washing the room in sterile blue light.

Only then did I see just how many cameras were pinned on us, and right below the screen was the plexiglass that separated us and the VIPs who'd been invited to watch the opening.

The theme song began to play through the crackling speakers, accompanied by the sound of bodies shifting anxiously.

Fucking Devil's Playground thinking they can force me in here like some type of animal.

But that's what they'd done for years, and no one could stop them. At least not *yet.* Not when they'd made so much money for the country that people were eating out of the palm of their dirty, bloody hands.

They could get away with *anything*.

Fuck, it wasn't even that long ago that murder had been illegal in literally any way.

They changed that. Fucked that up for all of us. Made made this world a living hell in the name of a game.

"Welcome, players, to Truth or Dare," a cheery, computer generated voice said as the screen cycled through all the contestants' faces and information. "This is the last of the Games this year, so we are looking forward to an *explosive* show."

That part was a jab at me, obviously. But it did make me smile.

Because, after all, while I might've been kidnapped and forced into the Game... it'd all been a part of my plan.

They came after me because *I* made them. They might've left me after they dealt with my mom, thinking I would be some naive little girl and move on with my life, too afraid to provoke them. Scurry away like a cockroach avoiding the kitchen light.

Fuck that.

I'd hacked into their computers and found out some of the vilest, dirtiest secrets I'd ever come across. Though, where they were keeping my mother was still out of my reach.

It was a risk putting me in the Games, but it was the only way they'd be legally able to kill me. Obviously, with power like theirs I could just *disappear*, but where was the fun in that? It simply wouldn't do for a fourth generation Legacy to vanish without a trace.

They didn't just want to kill me, they wanted to annihilate me. Destroy my family's reputation.

But it didn't matter.

Not only was I going to win Truth or Dare, but my entrance into the game would solidify the end of Devil's Playground forever.

THE STORY DOESN'T END HERE! LOOK FORWARD TO OUR NEXT RELEASE: TRUTH OR DARE TO SEE WHAT HAPPENS NEXT!

About Ashley

Bex (Ashley Pines) is a cat-mom of three, wife and spicy romance enthusiast living in Edmonton, AB. You can usually find her curled up on the sofa surrounded by a hundred pillows and reading on her kindle (or, y'know, writing.) Becoming her best friend is easy! You just need an undying love of all things sweet and be cool with watching the same five movies on repeat.

About Eden

Eden Emory is a contemporary spicy pen name for Elle Mae. This pen name will mostly focus on spicy dark wlw romance that pushes the boundaries and incorporates troupes normally seen in f/m romance.

Eden Emory was born out of a want for more. More spice, more wlw, and even more smutty vibes with little to no plot.

Loved this book? Please leave a review!

For more behind the scene content, sign up for my newsletter at https://view.flodesk.com/pages/61722d0874d564fa09f4021b